RELLIK

D1708246

RELLIK

TERESA MUMMERT

IN CHAOS THEORY, THE BUTTERFLY EFFECT IS THE SENSITIVE
DEPENDENCY ON INITIAL CONDITIONS IN WHICH A SMALL
CHANGE AT ONE PLACE IN A DETERMINISTIC NONLINEAR
SYSTEM CAN RESULT IN LARGE DIFFERENCES IN A LATER STATE.

ISBN: 1493738046
ISBN 13: 9781493738045

PROLOGUE

(PAST) FORSAKEN

Forsaken: abandoned or deserted.

I could still feel the warmth of her blood between my fingertips, my mind clouded in a heavy fog as thick as the syrupy substance on my hands. I stood over Katie, her face marred with dirt-stained tears as she stared off into nothingness. The leaves around us rustled as the wind blew hot against my back, the oppressive southern heat making it hard to breathe. If it weren't for the breeze I would have sworn that the Earth had frozen on its axis, suspending us in time. Heavy raindrops fell from the leaves, sending the crimson pool rippling around her still body.

"Katie, it's gonna be okay," I mumbled as I slid my hands under her back, lifting her from the dirt. Her body was limp and I struggled to stand as her head fell back, her long dark hair, slicked with blood hung in the freshly made mud from the late night Florida storm. "I'm so sorry. I'm so sorry."

I looped my other hand under her knees, my shoulder colliding hard with a tree as I pushed to my feet, bark biting into my flesh. I winced at the sudden burst of heat before my own superficial wound, but pain snapped me out of my daze and back into the moment. Time had not stilled for me, even if I would forever live in this moment.

Gritting my teeth, I began the long trudge out of the cover of the woods, our sanctuary turned hell. My muscles begged for reprieve but I continued on, determined to find help.

It felt like hours had passed since I took her into my arms and my muscles began to fail at the thought that it would be the last time. I placed her in the grass on the shoulder of Trails End Drive, pulling her ashy-toned face to my chest as I smoothed her hair from her cheek.

"I'm so sorry I got dirt in your hair," My words were strangled, my vision blurred as I looked into the lifeless eyes of the girl I loved. I'd never even said the words out loud to her.

Light illuminated her body as I felt her being pulled from my grip, but God couldn't take her. I still needed her here to be my angel. I held her close as hands ripped and clawed at my skin, desperate to pull her from my arms. My own body was being forced into the mud, as the silk of her hair slipped through my fingers.

"Call the police!" I watched the large silhouette holding her lifeless body walk away, blocking out the light momentarily. What I thought was Heaven was the headlight of a rusted blue pickup truck, God nothing more than a stranger. My angel had forsaken me. I closed my eyes as I quit struggling against the weight on my shoulders. There was no reason for me to fight anymore.

Chapter One

RELLIK (PRESENT)
AFTERMATH

AFTERMATH: THE PERIOD OF TIME AFTER A
BAD AND USUALLY DESTRUCTIVE EVENT

"You have a killer smile," The half-lit blonde with the perky tits slurred before tipping the bottle of bottom shelf vodka to her mouth.

"All the better to eat you with, my dear." I ran my tongue over my lips and smiled up at her as her hips swayed offbeat to the music. She giggled as she placed one knee beside me on the couch. I grabbed her hips to steady her as she straddled me.

"I can't believe I'm going to fuck Rellik fuckin' Bentley." She attempted to take another sip and I watched as vodka ran down her chin and pooled in her cleavage. Rolling my eyes, I jerked the bottle from her lips with more force than necessary.

"You won't be if you pass the fuck out on my lap, now will you?" I snapped.

She frowned as she put her hands on my shoulders and rolled her hips. "I'm sorry, baby," she purred. "Did I hurt your feelings?" Her fingers trailed along my jaw and I struggled to not pull back from her touch. Intimacy wasn't my strong suit.

"Hardly." I knocked her hand away and rested my head on the back of the couch, as the alcohol began to warm my body and quiet the memories.

"Can I kiss it make it better?" Her lips pressed against my chest and I let my eyes fall closed.

"If it will shut you up," I laughed as I slid my fingers into her hair tightened my grip, guiding her head lower. I didn't want her mouth on mine, it was a rule that was strictly adhered to.

They were all the same. Mindless whores willing to part their legs like the god damn Red Sea just to be able to say they fucked a guy in a band. But none of them really knew anything about me, and the hell that lived inside of my head. The rock star persona was a far cry from the man I really was. It was a shell. We weren't even fucking famous but it didn't stop the local groupies from throwing themselves at us. We had built a steady fan base in New Orleans and with the constant flow of tourists, our reputation had grown.

"You like that, baby?" The girl ran her tongue over her heavily glossed lower lip as she looked up at me through her fake lashes.

"I'm not your *fucking* baby. Do what you're here to do or get the fuck out."

She groaned and rolled her eyes but her mouth went back around my dick and she sucked as if her life depended on it. There was no secret as to what was happening here, she was using me to feel special and I needed to forget.

"Fuck," I mumbled as my fist tightened in her dry, bleached locks. My stomach muscles clenched as her tongue swirled under the head of my cock before my dick hit the back of her throat. She gagged and the reflex sent me over the edge. I came hard, holding her head in place to make sure she swallowed every last drop. She did so happily, wiping her pink acrylic nail under her mouth as she smiled up at me seductively.

"What about me?" She purred and just like that the high from coming evaporated, the ever-present memories returned.

"What about *you*?" My eyes narrowed as I zipped my jeans and ran my hand over my stomach.

"You're such a jerk," she snapped as she pushed to her feet and straightened her top.

"You're just figuring that out? It's a little late for modesty, don't you think?" My eyes drifted to her chest as she huffed and stormed off towards the door. "It was a pleasure," I called after her with a chuckle as it slammed behind her. I didn't play the game like other guys. I didn't give a fuck anymore about trying to impress women and get on their good side. There was no point. It wouldn't lead anywhere because there was nothing more I wanted then a good fuck and to be left alone. There was no challenge in the way they threw themselves at me.

I grabbed for the open bottle of Jack from the stand beside the couch and tipped it to my lips, letting the welcomed burn wash away another day. There was a tap at the door and it squeaked open as Trigger stuck his head inside.

"She didn't last long?" He smirked as he glanced over his shoulder.

"Neither did I," I quipped as I tipped the bottle up once more. Trigger shook his head, his caramel-colored hair falling into his eyes as his tongue piercing stuck out between his lips. Trig and I were polar opposites even though physically we could pass for brothers. I didn't have a single tattoo or piercing. He had more ink than a fucking paperback, but he was one of the few people in the world I would die for, even kill for. He was also the only one who knew what kind of hell I'd been through because he walked on the embers for most of his life.

He grabbed the bottle from my hand, laughing as it sloshed from the neck and onto my stomach. His dog tags clinked as he chuckled but there was no humor in his expression. Trigger had spent a few years in the Army after he became of age, but was honorably discharged after a misunderstanding with his sergeant that they chalked up to PTSD. The real story was something he never talked about and we all knew better than to bring it up.

"You're a fucking dick, man." I ran the palms of my hands over my face. I was drained from our concert and needing a good night of sleep, but I knew that was wishful thinking. I hadn't slept well since I was a teenager. Monsters loved to play in the dark. "Where are the guys?"

"Hangman is spending some quality time with those twins with the big tits and Phantom is on the prowl. This *is* New Orleans."

I nodded as I pushed to my feet. Phantom wouldn't be back until it was time for us to leave. This was his old stomping grounds and he has had some business to take care of on the outskirts of the French Quarter. I didn't ask him what that was he didn't offer up any information. We worked well that way. Playing this small time gigs brought in enough cash for gas money and to get is to the next set. That was more than enough for us because we had long given up on living and merely survived. Our dreams had died years ago, the idea of being famous no longer meant anything.

"Why are you lurking around here?" I stretched my arms over my head, groaning from my sore muscles. "Go get yourself some strange. What's the point of being in a band if you don't use it to get some ass?"

"Next week is Savannah. Gotta keep my head on a swivel." He said solemnly, the column of his throat bobbing as he swallowed hard but his face showed no emotion. "I want you guys with me when I visit Casey." I nodded, not knowing what to say. Trig was good at keeping that part of himself separate from our group. We'd all been avoiding the topic since the tour was planned out but going back was what Trig needed to get closure.

Trigger tipped the bottle to his lips and drank until he had no choice but to come up for air.

"You having second thoughts?" I asked as he sank down into the chair adjacent to the couch.

"Absolutely not." When Trig said he was going to do something, he made it happen. He was a man of his word and after a life of broken promises, it was remarkable to see him turn out so put together or maybe methodical would be a more accurate description. His eyes were so dark they were nearly black and after all he'd been through it gave him an inhuman quality, reflecting the monster he thought he was. But real monsters thrived in chaos, ruled by pain. Trigger was one of the good guys, whether he saw it or not.

"We can cancel Orlando and just go there for you. The guys won't mind." For the first time in years I was ready to face my past, but I was willing to wait if it helped Trig.

"So I'm not the only one trying to avoid the past." He shook his head and took another drink. I leaned forward and motioned for him to hand me the bottle, which he reluctantly gave me. Trigger had seen more carnage and horror than most can imagine, but war wasn't what caused him to suffer. His pain was who he was and it ate away at him like a cancer until he had no choice but to face it and it practically destroyed him. "No. Deviating from a plan is what gets people in trouble plus we'd run out of gas halfway there."

"This isn't Baghdad, Trig. You don't have to live by those rules anymore and I can make a few calls."

"Those rules kept my ass alive through a nine month deployment and I don't take handouts."

"I'm just saying you're not there anymore. You're not going back. That shit is over."

"Almost over. I need closure before I can move on."

"You think you'll be able to do that? Just forget it all?" I asked, genuinely curious.

"We don't have any other choice in life, do we? Suck it up and drive on." He shrugged. But being able to forgive and forget wasn't my strong suit. I was more of an eye for an eye type of man. The rules didn't apply to me.

CHAPTER TWO

RELLIK

RELLIK
BAD SEED

Bad Seed: a person who is seen as being congenitally disposed to wrongdoing and likely to be a bad influence on others.

The thing about sins is they don't have to be your own to haunt you. The sixth grade was the year I became obsessed with the classic rock my father would play in the garage while he worked on restoring his Barracuda. Pink Floyd and The Doors became part of the soundtrack to my life. I'd spent most of my free time coming up with my own lyrics, convinced one day my dad would be listening to me on the radio. I'd practice guitar, teaching myself the cords while my father shook his head and cursed under his breath in frustration. My life wasn't nearly as bad as I perceived it to be, but your scale is only weighted by your own experiences. Little did I know it was about to get heavy.

I sat in the back of class as Ms. Simmons held up a plastic cup full of dirt, a green stem topped by two leaves protruded from the rim. I stuck my pointer finger in my cup and felt around in the dirt for my seed that had failed to flourish but came up empty. I couldn't stop fidgeting. All I wanted to do was go home and see the guitar I was getting for my birthday. My eyes danced over Katie Alexander's hair that cascaded in dark waves over the back of her chair as she held up her cup to examine it. I reached out with dirty fingers and slid them between the silky strands. It was even softer than I had imagined. A lopsided grin spread across my face just as Katie turned, scowling in disgust and crumbling my spirit.

"Ew! You got dirt in my hair!"

So I did what any twelve year old boy would do when faced by his crush and impending humiliation, I gripped her hair tightly in my hand and yanked until she squealed. Fat, salty tears rolled over her pink cheeks as the entire room turned to glare at me and time froze to a painful halt.

My hand fell free from her tresses as I averted my gaze to my own cup of dirt on my desk. No emerald leaves grew like they had from the others. It was a bad seed, just like me. I'd watered it like I was told, turned the cup daily in the window sill to make sure it was getting the right amount of light, but like everything else I tried, I failed. But I refused to let anyone else know that I cared.

"Ryder, I have had enough of your disruptions." Ms. Simmons voice was stern but wavered as she spoke because I knew from her sad glances that she knew I was struggling. Her pity only made me more defiant. "Go down to Mr. Wallace's office."

The class collectively gasped and snickered at my misfortune, but I forced a smile and stood tall as I pushed from my old wooden desk. "Whatever," I mumbled under my breath as I knocked the plastic cup over and walked to the door. As I escaped into the desolate hallway, I toyed with the idea of leaving out of one of the side exits, but I knew an alarm would sound and I would probably end up in a lot more trouble. Reluctantly, I trudged on and entered the office. The secretary glanced over her wire-rim glasses before dropping her gaze back to her computer screen.

"To what do we owe the honor, Mr. Bentley?"

"Ms. Simmons hates me."

She snorted as she shook her head, her fingers clacking away against her keyboard. "Mr. Wallace is in with someone right now. Sit tight." She motioned with her chin to the three blue plastic chairs along the wall. I sat down, groaning as I kicked out my legs and looked over the motivational posters that hung on the wall.

My fingers tapped against my jeans to a classic rock song my father played on a loop as he worked on his car that never seemed to run just right. The secretary cleared her throat as she brushed back her fire-red curls from her face and my hand stilled.

"Can't have any fun in this place." The door to the principal's office opened as I spoke and I sat up straight, cutting off my words as an officer exited the room, stopping to turn to Mr. Wallace and say something.

His sullen eyes landed on mine and he stopped as he replied to the officer in a hushed tone and now both of them stared at me.

All I did was pull a stupid girl's stupid hair. My dad was going to kill me. Why did I have to touch her? Why couldn't I just be good like the others? Stupid girl. Stupid cake.

"Why are you here?" Mr. Wallace's eyebrows pulled together causing his forehead to crease.

"I uh… I don't know."

The men exchanged glances and I was waved into the office and told to sit. The police officer stood to my right as Mr. Wallace sat on the edge of his giant oak desk in front of me. He ran his hand along his jaw with a sigh as he avoided my gaze.

"I'm sorry," I blurted out as I felt my cheeks heat and my chest tighten.

"What?"

"I didn't think about the dirt on my fingers and then I was embarrassed," I rambled. When the cop placed his heavy hand on my shoulder I jumped fractionally and my pleas for forgiveness died in my throat and I held my breath, bracing for the punishment I had earned. Mr. Thomas, the guidance counselor and one of my mother's friends slipped inside the room. His eyes met Mr. Wallace's and he shook his head fractionally. "I got here as quickly as I could. I had some errands to run during my lunch break."

The officer sank down to eye level and ran his tongue over his lips and loudly cleared his throat. "There has been an accident."

"Ryder, Your father has been in an accident. He's at Reagan Memorial now and your mother is with him."

"Are they okay?" It felt as though someone had stomped on my chest. This was not the kind of surprise you expected on your birthday.

"Your mother is fine. She wasn't with your father at the time. The doctors are doing everything they can to help them." Mr. Thomas covered my dirty hand with his damp palm. I couldn't look him in the eye because it would only confirm that this was all real. Instead, I focused on the small bead of sweat clinging to his tanned flesh just below his auburn hair that was uncharacteristically disheveled. "She called me and asked for me to take you into the hospital."

My thoughts briefly drifted over his words and I had only absorbed one. "Them?"

He looked back at the officer before offering me a sad smile. "Grab your things. We can talk more on the road. Did you have lunch yet?"

I shook my head wondering how I could even eat after hearing something like this.

"I just finished my lunch at Franklin's deli when I got the call so we can stop at a drive-thru on the way." His hand slid from mine and he took a step back. I slowly stood and walked toward the door, with Mr. Thomas who following close behind me. The hall was still empty, something I normally loved because it felt like a different world without all of the people and noise, but now it felt small and suffocating. Tragedy has a way of putting life in perspective like that. I could smell the food from the cafeteria and it turned my stomach as I stopped in front of Ms. Simmons' door. I gripped the handle, shoving it wide open. The entire class sat silently, staring at me as I froze in the doorway. I felt utterly and devastatingly alone.

My skin was on fire and I could feel it dampen under my tears but I was unable to regain my composure. Still, the world continued to spin as I cried unabashedly. I'd just wanted to be noticed and now all I wanted was to disappear, evaporate. Kids whispered and giggled but I heard nothing but the steady whooshing of blood in my ears as *my heart raced. It felt like my veins had been electrified and I couldn't help but shuffle from one foot to the other. One set of eyes stayed locked on mine. Katie's expression mirrored my own sadness as she mouthed the words "Are you okay?" and I couldn't even find the strength to shake my head. Through blurred vision I stared down and smudged fingers and waited for Mr. Thomas to retrieve my book bag. No one else spoke a word to me and I wasn't even sure I was still breathing. All I could hear was my fears in rapid succession screaming inside of my head. Even in the moment of unknowing and panic I was able to take a lesson from Katie, even if it took me a few years to realize it. That moment of compassion when she owed me nothing changed something in me but there would be a lot more changes before the day would end.*

Mr. Thomas led me to his car and I slid into the old beige Buick, the heat from the day making it feel like I was in a sauna. As he got into the driver side, he tossed my book bag onto the back seat and offered me a sad smile.

"Everything is going to be okay," he said as he twisted the key in the ignition and the engine sputtered before growling to life. I pulled my seatbelt across my chest and clicked it into place.

"What happened," I asked knowing I wasn't prepared to hear the answer.

Mr. Thomas sighed as he adjusted his grip on the steering wheel and I focused on the rearview mirror. "I think I should leave that to your mother to explain." He glanced in the rearview mirror as he drove into the turning lane and headed towards the hospital.

We rode in silence, only speaking when he asked me what food I wanted from Shambles drive thru. I rambled off a number knowing I wouldn't be able to eat anything until I knew my dad was okay but maybe my mother would need something.

We parked near the emergency room entrance and I froze, suddenly terrified to know the truth that was on the other side of the automatic doors. In this moment he was neither alive nor dead. We were suspended in a state of unknowing and I wanted to stay there for as long as possible. My father was everything to me.

Mr. Thomas got out of the car and came to my side, pulling open the door for me. I hesitated, hating that in such a vulnerable moment I had to force back my tears so I could be strong for my mother. I pushed myself out of the car, paper bag of food in hand, and towards the automatic doors that read EMERGANCY in red-lighted lettering.

Mr. Thomas kept his hand on my shoulder as he guided me from the waiting area to a set of heavy thick wooden doors. He hit the button on the wall and they opened before me. The site of doctors and patients hurrying through the mint colored hall filled my view.

"Your mother is in the third room to the left. I have to wait out here, but if you need me just come back through these doors." He looked up and I noticed that a nurse in pink scrubs stood to my side. He nodded to her and she placed her hand on my shoulder. I wanted to shrug her away but I didn't have any energy. She guided me to the waiting room that was nothing more than a hole in the wall with a few blue vinyl chairs lining the walls.

When her puffy, tear soaked eyes met mine she sobbed into a tissue she had pressed against her mouth, her freshly honey-highlighted hair knotted and disheveled. I'd never seen my mother cry. She was always so happy or at least that was the illusion I had become accustomed to. I felt like I was on autopilot, unable to think or feel. I was thankful for the numbness that had taken over because my mother was in no state to comfort me. She lurched toward me, wrapping her arms around my shoulder and squeezing me with all of her strength. She pulled back, her hands on my face and frantically rubbing my hair as if she was examining me to make sure I was okay.

"I brought you food," I mumbled, realizing how stupid it was to think a chicken sandwich would somehow take away her pain, but I wasn't ready to hear about my father's condition.

She smiled, her hand still trying to tame my hair as she sniffled. "I had lunch at Frankin's Deli, but you should eat something, baby."

CHAPTER THREE

OVERWHELM

Overwhelm: Defeat completely.

I rubbed my damp palms over my jeans as I looked over the printed newspaper clippings that hung from push-pins across my faded yellow bedroom wall. The time-line dated back ten years to when I was only eight years old. I'd never been this close to finding out the truth and it was nearly overwhelming. After losing most of my research after a break-in, I had almost given up, but thanks to the internet and the local library I was able to rebuild my paper trail with a few new clues along the way. My own personal memories began much younger, when my world began to crumble and the wheels of fate began to spin.

"I don't want to go to grandmas. She's mean and makes me eat peas." I rubbed the back of my hand across my nose as I sniffled, struggling to hold back tears. Momma always fought to be tough for me and I owed her the same. I knew this wasn't what she wanted to do, like going to the doctors, but it was important because it kept me healthy.

"Don't think of it that way, baby. Think of it as… you're Cinderella and you have to go stay with your fairy god-mother for a while." My mother was on edge, constantly glancing out of my bedroom window and she gathered a few of my things. My dresser drawers were left open and clothing strewn about the floor. It felt like goodbye, one of the many times we'd run in the middle of the night, but this time was different. I wasn't going to be by my mother's side, I was being left behind. It stung in a way I had never felt before and couldn't quite understand.

"But she's an evil stepmother."

My mother ran her hand through my long, mahogany-colored hair and smiled sadly, her eyes glossed over in unshed tears.

"Then you can be Belle."

"But I don't like to read," I groaned as I clung to my doll baby whose hair was a matted knot the same color as my own and her leg had fresh blue stitching from my mother repairing it.

"Sweetheart, you can be anyone you want to be, okay? Just like last time. Anyone you want but we have to go."

"But daddy said he'd come be with us soon!"

"Ella, when did you talk to your father?"

I shrugged as I fixed the yarn hair of my homemade doll, pulling at one of the many knots. "He came to day care and said he would come to be with us soon."

"Oh, Ella. Sweetie, you have to tell me if your daddy comes to see you. Remember? We talked about this." I could hear the disappointment in her voice, but her smile didn't waver.

"He said it was a surprise for you!" I groaned.

She shook her head. She looked upset and I was worried she was mad at me for ruining the secret.

"Daddy wants you to go too. He knows it is the best thing for you right now."

"You talked to daddy?" I couldn't contain my excitement. It felt like it had been a lifetime since we were all together, after the cops came and took daddy away to help them get more of the bad guys. My daddy was a hero. He promised me he would come back for us and we would be a family again when his job was done. But momma hated having to wait for him and would always move us around a lot.

"I'll tell you all about it on the way."

I gathered my long, stick-straight dark hair into a ponytail, pulling an elastic band from my wrist and secured it in place as my eyes danced over the clues. My story wasn't an uncommon one. A lot of kids get put in the system and never get a reason as to why their lives had been turned upside down. But mine had a twist and I couldn't shake the feeling that there was something sinister lying just below the surface of the details. My father was a criminal and my mother was a thief, even if she struggled to keep that reality from me. But it's hard to keep a secret as big as ours.

"It's just for a few weeks. I never ask you for anything."
I listened to my mother plead with my grandma outside of the cracked passenger window of her old blue Sundance.

"What have you gone and gotten yourself into now?" My grandmother folded her arms over her chest as she narrowed her eyes behind thick, clear-rimmed glasses.

"She's your granddaughter. Don't you have any compassion?"

"Don't you have any sense of responsibility? You get yourself all pear shaped and expect the world to come to your side, save the day. I told you Tommy was going to ruin your life. That man never cared about anyone but himself. Who is here to help me when I need it? I'm not young anymore, Leigh. You don't see me asking for a handout."

"Here." My mother pulled a stack of money from her back pocket and held it out.

"Where did you get this?" My grandmother asked but my mom shoved the money into her hand and folded her fingers over the stack of bills.

"She can help you. She loves to help cook and she picks up after herself. She's a good kid, Ma. Just look at her." My mother stretched out her arm in my direction and my grandma's expression softened momentarily before she glared back at my mother. "I just need a little time. Someone's been leaving me messages, Ma. I think it's Tommy."

"I've always had to clean up your messes. The first time that man stepped through the door, your father should have put him to ground. God rest his soul." She turned and made her way up the wooden steps into her apartment, gripping the railing to steady herself. "Always mixed up with the law. Do you even care how the neighbors look at me? Of course you don't. You only care about yourself."

My mother spun around and pulled open my door, a fresh reassuring smile on her face as she reached across me and unbuckled my seatbelt. "Come on, baby. You're grandma is excited to spend some time with you."

I weakly smiled back but my heart sank as I took my mother's hand and let her lead me up the stairs. I stopped *in the doorway, hiding myself behind her legs as I eyed my grandmother in a faded mauve recliner.*

"Don't be scared. I won't bite you," she said as she pressed her nurse-style shoes against the brown carpet to rock herself.

"Thank you, ma. I promise this is temporary." My mom knelt down beside me, cupping my cheeks in her palms. She smiled, a small sob escaping her as she fought against her tears. "You be good, okay?" She sniffled but her smile grew brighter. "I'll be back soon. I promise."

"I forgot magic shield!"

"Do her a favor, Leighton and don't bother," My grand-mother interjected as my mother pressed her lips to my forehead.

"It's okay. You won't need it here. No more nightmares. I love you. Take care of that baby doll for me, okay?" She ran her hand over my hair before stepping out of the door and my life forever.

My mother had always loved me. My every memory I had of her was of smiles and warm embraces, even when the world was against her. But memories are subjective when you're young and idolize those who show you affection. She told me she would be back for me. That was what I clung to all of these years, even after my grand-mother passed away and there was no one else to take me in. I would walk to the ends of the earth to find out why she never returned, if my father had finally caught up with her. But the real tragedy began after I'd lost everyone I knew and now I was desperate for answers and a resolu-tion so I could move on with my life.

I sighed as I sunk down on the edge of my bed and pulled my knees to my chest. My apartment was barely the size of an average bedroom but it served its purpose and I didn't plan on staying much longer. If my leads didn't work out in Orlando, I'd have to figure out another way to get information. I didn't have much but I didn't need much. The light at the end of my tunnel was the truth. It was what I had in my darkest moments. I wasn't that small, helpless child in a foster home anymore. I had grown stronger, learned to overcome and now I could protect myself like my mother could not.

After running away from an abusive family and being thrown back into foster care, I walked free on a technicality known as adulthood. When you go into the system, it's impossible to escape but eventually you age and get thrown out with little hope of surviving and becoming a productive citizen. I clung to the stories I had learned as a child. One day the world will right itself, justice will be served and a hero will save the day. I wasn't that little girl anymore. I was my own God damn hero and I was going to make things right.

I grabbed my messenger bag from my bedside table and shoved my old ratty baby doll inside that my mother had sewn from a cloth glove. It was ratty and the yarn hair was falling out, but it was all I had. Climbing on my bed I slowly took down each piece of newspaper and stuck them inside my purse. It made me feel safer knowing that I kept the most important things by my side since I hadn't been able to pay my rent this month and I wasn't on a lease. I left my bedroom, shutting off the light behind me. I had ten minutes before my shift started at Crowley's Bar and I couldn't afford to lose my job. Locking the door behind me, I left my apartment and descended into the night muggy night. I loved working night shifts. There was something anonymous about being cloaked in darkness, mingling in the shadows, never having to reveal your true self. It was freeing. I never craved to be center of attention, in the spotlight.

At the bar I was the fun girl who loved loud music and giving relationship advice to the sloppy drunks. They loved to flirt and tell me how pretty my smile was, none being able to see it was a façade. I wasn't a miserable person, don't get me wrong. I was just very focused and driven.

I lived only five minutes from the bar so I didn't need to worry about buying a car or wasting money on a cab. I could take the alley way behind my apartment building and cut across Long Street to the back entrance. I had been in Orlando for nine weeks but this place wasn't home. Nowhere felt like home and I knew that wouldn't change until I found answers and could put my past to rest.

The alley smelled of urine and car exhaust and I did my best to hold my breath as I slipped into the backdoor of the club.

"Cutting it close, Ella," Maric shook his head as he wiped a rag over the bar, his thick dark hair hanging down into his eyes.

"I'm sorry. I got held up. My cat was sick and I had to clean up the hairball," my voice trailed off as he stared at me. "Fine. I lost track of time."

"You want to lose your job?"

"A dream job like this?" I rounded the bar as he glared at me and handed me the rag.

"A job is a job is a job and my money spends the same as anyone else's."

"Yeah, but your money gest shoved into disease infested crotch first."

"I'd shove a few bills into your granny panties if you get up on that pole."

I grabbed a lemon and began cutting it into wedges. "Not a chance in hell."

Maric winked at me before tapping his palm against the counter. "I like a girl who plays hard to get."

"Ugh, you like anything with a pulse," I groaned as I dropped the slices into the plastic bin and grabbed another. "In fact, I'd bet money you'd hit anything before rigor mortis set in."

"The offer stands if you ever change your mind about dancing."

"This job is only temporary," I mumbled to myself as Maric walked away.

"It's been five years, Leigh. You said this was only temporary and now I'm raising your child," My grandmother spoke into the phone as she stirred a pot of chicken noodle soup on the stove. I sat in the center of the living room floor trying to comb out my baby doll's hair with my fingers. "I can't send you any money if that's what you want. I am barely getting by on my social security. I can't even afford my meds for this month."

There was a pause in the conversation and I pretended I wasn't listening.

"What sort of trouble?" My grandma put her hand over the receiver and called out to me, "Mikaella, go fetch me my glasses from beside my bed."

I reluctantly got up from the floor and made my way to the stairs. I climbed them as fast as I could to retrieve her glasses and when I returned, I crept quietly halfway down and sat on a step so I could listen to their conversation.

"School will be starting again soon. She needs shots and supplies." Grandma groaned and I could picture her shaking her head in disapproval. "What do I tell her when other kids bring up that her mother is a criminal? Or that her father is insane? What then? She is going to have to live with what you've done for the rest of her life." She listened to my mother before responding to whatever she had said.

"I don't want any more of your money. I want you to grow up and take care of your daughter."

I stood up, rubbing my damp eyes with the back of my hand and slowly descended the steps. My grandmother looked me over, her eyes sad.

"Come say hello to your mother, Mikaella."

I walked across the living room and into the kitchen. Grandma took her glasses and held out the beige phone. Reluctantly, I took it from her hand, twisting my body in the long cord as I cleared my throat.

"Baby, are you there?" My mother's voice sounded rough as if she was fighting a cold.

"I don't want to start school," I whispered.

"Don't you worry about that. I'll be coming for you real soon, okay?"

"Okay."

"I'm really sorry I missed your birthday. Nine years old! You're practically a grown up. I got you a present."

"You found daddy," I asked as I twisted the phone cord around my fingers.

"No, baby. A new magic shield just like your old one. Are you still having those nightmares?"

"Sometimes." I shrugged as I thought about the sleepless nights.

"Baby, I have to go," her voice was panicked and it sounded like she had moved away from the phone. "I have to go. I love you." The line went dead before I could respond. That was the last time I'd ever heard from my mother.

Chapter Four

RELLIK
LOYALTY

Loyalty: A strong feeling of support or allegiance.

Humans by nature are pack animals. We take comfort in those around us, and value our worth by how many others deem us important. We struggle to fit in, be like the others.

I now had a few that I would call family, but our loyalty comes from understanding the true depravity of human nature, not from blood. Although, blood had been shed to bring us together and more would be shed when we were torn apart.

"We have to go," Phantom kicked my leg and I groaned, rubbing my hand over my stubbled jaw as I stretched.

"Fuck you," I growled as he clicked a button on the remote and dropped it on the table in front of me causing Trigger to startle awake.

"You fucking prick!" Trig was on his feet, alert but his eyes were vacant and it took a few seconds for him to come back to reality. He turned and rammed his shoulder against Phantom's as he shoved by him. Phantom was twice as wide as the rest of us but built out of pure muscle.

"You know you can't fucking do shit like that when he's sleeping." I stood and stretched, my muscles tight from a night of drinking, wishing I could fall into a perpetual sleep so I'd never have to leave Katie behind for the harsh reality of everyday life. No matter how many people thought I was a fuck up, she always saw something good in me, even if it wasn't really there.

"It's time to go, man." Much like Trig, Phantom's problems began early but it wasn't about who he was, but who he wasn't. Sometimes there are worse things than being beaten and abused. Abandoned and neglected he saw the world in black and white, compassion and empathy are things he doesn't possess. Only good or evil. Misery loves company and that is why we all gravitated towards each other.

I nodded and gathered my things before following him out in to the harsh sunlight and into the large black SUV parked just outside of the door. We didn't travel in a bus because it was a luxury we couldn't yet afford.

I climbed in the driver's seat as Hangman got into the passenger side of the black Durango, mid- conversation talking about his night. I adjusted the rearview mirror.

"Them twins had some tig ole' bitties, man. I'm surprised she didn't give me a black eye."

"You're lucky the boyfriend didn't give you one either," Trig laughed as Hang turned around to glare at him.

"How the fuck was I supposed to know the dumb one had a boyfriend?"

"The dumb ones always do," Phantom chimed in as I pulled out onto the road.

"Then why is Trig single?" Hangman laughed a Trig smacked him in the back of his head.

"Fuck you, you fucking prick."

I ignored them, drowning out their conversation with heavy rock blasting from the radio as we headed down the road, the GPS navigating us to Orlando, Florida, the place I used to call home. The idea of stepping foot in my home town made my skin crawl. This was our life. Every day was the same. Most thought what we did was glamorous but in truth it was long nights filled with highway and strangers. The hours rolled by, weeks, months and it felt like we never really went anywhere. My mind was lost in my past, an endless loop much like my life now.

"Why aren't you answering my calls?"

I glanced up from the fallen tree I leaned against to see Katie standing before me in her ivory church dress. At sixteen she was still the beautiful girl I couldn't help but stare at, only now she had grown three inches and her curves had filled out. I shrugged and continued to dig my father's pocket knife into the sole of my black Adidas shell top sneaker.

"You know you can talk to me, Ryder."

"It's the 23rd," I mumbled before shoving the knife harder into the shoe.

"Oh," She sat down beside me, not worrying about ruining her dress. "Right. The 23rd." I glanced over at her, her hair pulled up in a bun with a few loose curls. I didn't need to explain what I meant. Katie and I had been hanging out together ever since my father died, even more now since her mom got remarried. It had been four years since

the accident, but the anniversary of that day brought me back to that moment like not a single hour had passed. He was such a great man, never did anything wrong and one day everything about his image was shattered.

"Give me your hand."

I eyed her suspiciously but held out my hand to her. She placed a small hand-made bracelet, woven from thin black and blue plastic strips, over my wrist.

"That make it better?" She pressed her lips to my temple and all of the pain evaporated under her touch. "Happy birthday, Ryder."

"Why do you have your hair up like that?" I made a face at her and she giggled. "You know I love it when you wear it down."

She folded her arms over her chest as she stuck her chin in the air defiantly. "To keep mean boys with dirty fingers from pulling it."

I fought against a smirk but I couldn't help it. "No mean boys will ever pull your hair again or they will have to deal with me."

"You're the meanest of them all," She quipped. "What's that?" She pointed to the torn wrapping paper on the ground beside me. I picked up the small key ring and held it in front of me. "It's for my car."

"You're kidding?" She was more excited than I had been, but seeing her smile made it all worth it.

"The Barracuda my dad was restoring before he died," my voice trailed off as my throat became thick with sadness.

"I think it's sweet." We fell silent as she reached up and touched one of the tiny feathers that hung from the bottom. "When do I get to see your car?"

"My mom thinks I'll be ready to take my test soon but the car still needs a lot of work. I never really paid attention when dad was trying to teach me all of that car stuff."

"You're smart. You'll teach yourself." She rubbed her fingers over a light purplish spot on her arm.

"What's that?"

"Bryce was being a jerk this morning because I took too long in the bathroom before church. I miss being an only child." She shrugged but I knew she hated her step-brother.

"You want me to kick his ass?"

Her eyes lit up but she shook her head but she was fighting to hide a smile. *"That won't make anything better."*

I closed the knife and stuck it in my tin pencil box that I kept hidden in a hole of our favorite tree. Taking Katie's hand in mine, she watched me suspiciously as I slowly raised her hand and pressed my lips against the bruise. "How about that?"

"Much better."

"What about this," I asked as I leaned over and pressed my lips against hers. Her fingers slid over the side of my neck as her lips parted and my tongue swept over cherry flavored lips.

"Jesus Christ, Rellik. Stop fucking daydreaming and watch the God damn road!" Phantom's deep voice pulled me from my memories. I blinked away the sad faces and checked the GPS to make sure we were still making good time. My eyes met his briefly in the rearview mirror and I knew he was worried but I had everything under control, always. I watched the road ahead, glancing down at my hand on the steering wheel and still seeing the dirt covered fingers and back to the tiny drops of water that splattered against the windshield. It was hard to push the past away as we grew closer to where it all happened. This trip was going to test the limits of all our sanity. I wished I could rid my mind of the memories but my whole life was a walking nightmare.

"I'm fine," I replied, my throat feeling tight and I struggled to clear it. "Just hung over." Reaching for the dial, I turned up the volume and clicked to play our CD that was already in the player, in hopes of drowning out my thoughts, but the voices couldn't be quieted. They were a part of who I was now, Katie's memories a constant reminder of what I could never have.

> **Bitter sympathy was all she offered me,**
> **Warm and tempting, her glass half empty,**
> **She poured herself out, judgment under cloud,**
> **I drank her all in, my secret sin**
> **Pain fades fast when I got my whiskey glass**

From the back passenger side, Trigger reached forward and bumped my shoulder with a bottle of water. "Hydrate. Stay alert, stay alive," he mumbled and I took the bottle with a nod and drank two-thirds of the contents before taking a deep breath as the chilled water alleviated the pressure in my throat. I tossed the container on the passenger floor and Hangman smacked my arm with the back of his hand and laughed, the tension easing in my chest as I slowly pushed my memories to the dark corner of my mind to ignore for another day. Of all of us, Hangman was the only one with both feet on the ground, ironic considering how he had come to earn his name. Drug-induced psychosis was enough to leave anyone hanging from a thread, or an extension cord in his case.

We all had our demons. Some flesh and bone, others chemical but they tortured us each just the same. Life wasn't about living to the fullest, for some, for us, it was about surviving. No one gave a fuck about the events that brought us together, they only wanted to be entertained, but music for us was an escape. It was the blood that oozed from the wound. Same struggle, different demons.

I clicked next on the CD player and a slower ballad began to play, one that I had written when I was fifteen. Katie's parents were extremely strict and it was no secret that I wasn't what anyone would want for their daughter. Even I knew I was wrong for her but I couldn't keep myself away and she refused to give up on me.

Does the mirror lie, as you hold my hand?
Or do my secrets hide, conceal the man.
Because I can't give you what you need.
My hands are dirty, Baby, you're so clean.
Falling for the wrong was your mistake.
Giving me your heart for me to break.

I listened to myself playing the acoustic guitar over the radio and Hangman tapped his fingers on his leg. Drumming to him was as vital as his heartbeat.

"It's kind of depressing," Katie scrunched her nose as she read the notebook page over my shoulder.

"Life is depressing." I covered the page with a sigh. "I wrote that one last year anyway."

"Oh, come on. Things aren't that bad. Pretty soon Mr. Thomas won't be breathing down you neck anymore and reporting your every move back to your mom," she said with a laugh.

"Yeah, I'm so glad they've transferred him. It's hard to have any fun with your stepdad around."

"I know that feeling." Her expression fell and I dropped my pen to pull her across my lap.

"What's up with that guy? You act like he's the devil or something. I thought everyone loved coach."

She shrugged as she snuggled in against my chest and traced the lettering of my t-shirt. "He's just a jerk. He's always following me around and yelling at me. Of course he thinks his son is never wrong. I can't wait to get out of that freaking place."

"Where do you think we should go after graduation?"

She lifted her head to look up at me, her cheeks burning red as she fought against a smile. "You're planning on coming with me when I leave this town?"

"Of course. I'd follow you anywhere." I placed my fingers under her chin and pressed my lips against hers. "Or you could follow me when I'm super famous. Someone is going to have to keep the girls away." I shrugged.

She smacked me on the chest playfully and laid back against me. "No way. It's you and me. No one else."

"No one else." Rubbing my hand over her knee I pressed my cheek against the top of her head and closed my eyes. Katie had no idea how much she had helped me after my dad died. I owed her everything. If she asked me to leave this place today I'd do it without a second thought.

"Pinky promise?" She raised her hand with her pinky finger extended.

"What?"

"*Pinky promise me that it's only us. Forever.*" I wrapped my arms tightly around her and fell back on the grass, pulling her over on top of me.

"*Why do you have to be such a girl?*"

"*I am a girl,*" Giggling she squirmed to get away from me as I tickled my fingers over her ribs.

"*My girl.*"

She pulled the notebook from between us and I stretched my arm out to take it back, but she held it away as she tried to sit up.

"*You better give that back,*" I yelled, laughing as I tickled her, causing her to giggle as she flipped the book open.

"*You're always writing in this thing. I want to see what you say about me.*" She flipped the book open and I stopped tickling her as she began to read. My heart racing as she read my most intimate thoughts about her. There was hardly ever a time Katie wasn't on my mind and for reasons unknown, she enjoyed spending time with me. We never talked about what we had between us, our relationship just evolved naturally and neither of us labelled it. We just were us and no one else came between us.

After a moment she closed the notebook and turned around to face me. "*You're really good, Ryder.*"

Chapter Five

ELLA

Sanctuary: a place of refuge or safety.

"Shifts over, Maric," I called to the end of the bar where my boss sat on a stool with a shot of tequila in hand. He nodded but finished talking to one of the patrons as I cashed out my drawer.

I smiled and feigned interest as a couple of men tried to start a casual conversation with me, but my mind was lost in my own world. My imagination had become my sanctuary because it was the only place I had ever had control. I moved on to counting my tips, which were few and far between. Men saved their singles for those nearly naked dancers over the frumpy girl who poured their drinks. Maric had worked his way down the bar and was now standing across from me.

"You want to get together later?" He always asked the same question and I always turned him down, something that didn't happen often to him. But like any man, he was predictable and wanted what he couldn't have. He saw me as a challenge.

"It does feel a little chilly in here. Has hell frozen over?"

He smiled, loving my unfiltered mouth, but I saw him tense as the trucker sitting across the bar laughed at him. "Something funny?"

I laughed as Maric walked me to the back door and held it open for me to exit. I wrapped my hand in my purse strap nervously. I glanced around the desolate alley as I prepared to leave the safety of the club into darkness. "I was thinking more along the lines of… a deal."

"What kind of deal," he asked leaving his expression unreadable. But I could get a good sense of his mood by the tone of his voice. He was intrigued and perhaps a little amused. "You want to be my bottom bitch? You're gonna hafta up your game." He slid his fingers through my hair and I cringed at the smell of stale cigarettes. "You can't be looking like some frumpy housewife."

"No," I swatted his hand away and took a step backwards "I need more money. I could help you with some manager responsibilities or pick up some extra shifts."

"A raise? For what? Raise a few dicks and we'll talk about money." He was crass but that was something that didn't faze me anymore. I wasn't raised to be lady-like, I wasn't raised at all, just kept alive.

"Come on, Maric. I work twice as hard as anyone here and you know that. I'm about to lose my apartment and you'll just have to train someone to take my place when I'm left on the street."

His eyes travelled down my body and I resisted the urge to gag at his repulsive expression. He chuckled, shaking his head. "I already gave you the extra shift tonight. I can't afford to throw cash at you. The economy is shit, Ella. My hands are tied. Go change. Be back here in twenty minutes looking a little more human. And get something to eat! Don't think I haven't noticed you eating all the cherries and shit. This ain't a soup kitchen."

"Human. Got it." I beamed as he shook his head and disappeared into the alley, the relentless heat still hanging in the air, even long after sunset. I must have looked homeless, but it all helped perpetuate the image of helplessness. No one looked twice at the poor, frail girl and I was happy to be left alone. Maric acted like a dirty old man, but he was no different from any other man. He couldn't resist a sad pout and the opportunity to ride in and save the day. But they always wanted something in return and that wasn't a price I was willing to pay.

I was bouncing with each step as I made my way towards my apartment until I saw the eviction noticed taped to my door and a padlock hung from the frame. "Fuck," I groaned as I grabbed my hair in frustration. I hurried back down the stairs and into the alley alongside my building.

After a few jumps I grabbed onto the metal fire escape and pulled it down to the road.

I climbed it quickly, hurrying past my neighbor's window and to my apartment. My bedroom window had several coats of paint and the lock no longer turned. I struggled to lift it and slipped inside. I changed as quickly as possible into a short, jean skirt and a tight pale blue tank top trimmed in lace. I glanced around the small space but there was nothing I needed to salvage. A few outfits were all I had and they were dirty. I shoved them into an old blue backpack before hurrying back down the fire escape toward work. I didn't have time to worry about what I would do tonight.

From behind me I heard someone catcall, their shoes fast approaching on gravel. I held up my middle finger as I continued on, struggling to walk gracefully in my wedge sandals. I was in no mood for that kind of bullshit.

"Aww, don't be that way, baby. Whatchya' got in your bag? You holding?"

"Go fuck yourself." I called out as I yanked the hairtie from my hair, wincing as it ripped a few strands. My own pain was a momentary distraction that afforded the stranger time to get dangerously close without my noticing.

"What the fuck you say?" Large, calloused fingers wrapped around my throat, squeezing effortlessly as the smell of tequila wafted over my face. "You got an ugly tongue for such a pretty girl."

I dug my fingernails into the back of his hand until the pressure on my throat eased fractionally. "You've got an ugly fucking face." I swung my leg wildly, begging to connect with his groin as my heart pounded against my chest, threatening to explode. I worked out daily, had taken self-defense classes but nothing really prepares you for the real thing.

"You have a big set of balls thinking you can talk to me like that, bitch."

"I just have nothing to lose." I shoved against his shoulder with as much force as I could muster as his hand came down across my face. In an effort to avoid the blow he had caught the left side of my forehead, his ring biting into my flesh and I yelled as I struggled to put a few inches of distance between us.

"Wrong, bitch. You have your life."

Chapter Six

RELLIK
SACRIFICE

Sacrifice: the act of giving up something that you want to keep especially in order to get or do something else or to help someone.

I waited outside of the door, breathing in the humid night air as I waited for Phantom to come out. The door opened and Phantom slapped his palm against mine and I held up the little plastic bottle filled with pills he had handed to me. I slipped the drugs into my pocket with a nod of approval as shouting from across the alley got our attention. We were illuminated by an old street lamp that bathed us in yellow.

"I love it when a plan comes together," I joked as I struggled to see what was happening in the dark.

"We need to rehearse, man, it's already nine," Phantom snapped, making it clear he knew what I was thinking and didn't approve.

I glanced back at him with my arms extended. How could we just walk away? Phantom's jaw clenched and I knew this would be an argument later. But he didn't understand why any of us cared about anyone outside of our group.

"Hold my bail money." I pulled a wad of bills from my pocket and shoved it against Phantom's chest along with my wallet.

"Oh, hell no. Don't do this man. We have a fucking show," He yelled after me, his deep gravelly voice causing a cat to take off across the alleyway. I ignored him as I pulled my Pink Floyd t-shirt over my head, adrenaline causing my heart to race.

"I'm about to give you a show!"

I crossed the alley and was behind the large man that towered over a frightened woman. His finger were around her throat and she was using the last of her breath to curse him. Tapping him on the shoulder he spun around and eyed me up. He was a good half foot taller than me but I learned how to take care of myself young.

"What the fuck do you want, pussy?" He sneered, his face red with anger. I took a step closer and looked him square in the eye. I never showed fear, never backed down.

"My turn."

He widened his stance and chuckled, the smell of stale liquor wafting off him. "Go home, boy." He dismissed me with a wave of his hand and turned back to the girl. I rolled my neck and glanced over my shoulder to Phantom who shook his head. I shoved my palm hard against his shoulder, causing him to almost lose his balance before spinning back around to face me.

"I fucking," his words cut off with a guttural groan as I swung a wide right hook and connected with his left cheek bone. He stumbled backwards and the woman squealed as he collided with her. She jumped and took a few steps back as the man touched his face before examining the smattering of blood on his fingers. "You fucking son of," My next blow hit his stomach and he doubled over as the air left his lungs in a rush. He stood quick and lurched for me, I dodged his grasp and tossed my shirt to the girl. She caught it as she stood frozen just feet from us.

"A big guy like you who likes to man-handle women should be tougher than this. I'm kind of disappointed." I joked, my body humming with the rush of endorphins. "Show me what you got, pussy." I goaded him and his lip twitched as he took a large stride towards me. He swung with his left, catching me off guard. His knuckled collided with my jaw and my mouth filled with the metallic taste of my own blood as my lip split inside against my teeth. I grinned as I wiped the pad of my thumb over the dampness.

"That's disappointing."

Tires squealed from a few streets over, distracting my opponent, and giving me the opening I needed. I stepped forward and swung with my left than right and he hit the gravel, catching himself on his elbows. I was over him immediately, taking advantage of his disorientation. I felt his nose pop and the bones give under my busted knuckles. I was blinded by rage and the muffled cried of the woman only caused me to slip deeper. In my own head were flashes of Katie as she sobbed, begging not to tell a soul the despicable secrets I had uncovered. The look of terror in her young eyes caused me to snap.

I paced the ground, gripping my hair in my fists as I struggled to calm myself. The foundation only partially hid the small purpling cut on her cheekbone.

"He didn't mean to," her voice trailed off as she wiped her cheek with the palm of her hand. "He just gets a little high and doesn't think."

"Didn't mean to? Are you fucking kidding me," I yelled before huffing out a breath and begging myself to calm down. It wasn't Katie I was mad at, it was her fucking stepbrother who had decided to get handsy with her at one of his parties. But she slipped up and admitted that it wasn't the first time and I knew it wouldn't be the last if I didn't do something. "If he ever," I shook my head, my eyebrows pulled together as I tried to think clearly. "If he touches you again," I stepped in front of Katie who stood from the fallen tree log and put her hands on my chest. I'd never felt so much anger inside of me. The small fights between them I could handle but knowing he had tried to hurt her, violate her had sent me over the edge.

"I'll tell you, I promise."

"I'll fucking kill him." I clenched my teeth until they hurt. I didn't want to wait. He deserved to pay for what he had done to her.

"If my parents find out I'm seeing you they won't let me out of the house. I can't lose you and I'll be stuck in there with him."

"Then leave with me. I have my license now and I've been saving money."

"Ryder, you know we can't do that. How would we live? Where would we stay?"

"I can't let him hurt you again, Katie. I can't."

I turned to walk away, determined to make things right. As her fingertips slid from my chest I felt my heart sink into my stomach. The idea of not being able to see her *again was agonizing but in the moment it felt like I had no other option.*

"Please don't do this, Ryder. Please," Her voice shook under her words as I continued to make my way through the trees. I had no choice. When you love someone you sacrifice. I would give her up if it saved her. "You can't tell anyone."

I kept walking, my feet feeling heavy and my heart crumbling. She may not understand now but she will thank me later.

"Please stop," her voice echoed through the trees as her words faded.

The teenage mind only works on two levels. We were either complacent or discontent. After finding out that Bryce had tried to touch my girlfriend, his own stepsister, I was a motherfucking animal. I wanted to soak my hands in his blood and make him cry. I wanted him to hurt like he had hurt my Katie. The consequences of my actions never crossed my mind. I only wanted to make things right.

I had no memory of my trip to her home. I knocked on her front door hard enough to split one of my knuckles. Bryce opened the door with a look of confusion before he smiled.

"You decided to join the team."

"What?" It took me a moment to remember his father was the football coach. He had asked me several times to tryout but organized sports wasn't my thing. I didn't play well with others.

"Dad's upstairs. One sec." He turned and called for his father and I knew I didn't have much time to make my point. "Unless you're here for my sister. I see you guys talking in the hall sometimes. You hittin' that?"

"What happened there?" I eyed the two scratch marks that crept out of his shirt collar and up his neck.

"Practice." He was nonchalant but I knew his injury didn't come from football. His practice would eventually lead to the rape of Katie. I closed my fist and shoved it hard into Bryce's stomach causing him to grunt as he doubled over, struggling to breathe.

I used the advantage to slam my elbow into the back of his head, causing him to fall on the concrete steps that lead to his door. He groaned and pushed himself up with one hand. I kicked, my foot hitting under his chin, sending him sprawled on his back.

"Yeah, I'm here for Katie." I grabbed his face and slammed his head down on the cement. He gripped the sleeves of my shirt, clawing at my biceps as I did it again and again.

His blood pooled on the concrete steps as my body shook from the rush of adrenaline. "Not so fucking tough now, are you?" He let out a few chocked sobs.

"Next time I'm going to kill you." I hit him again in the jaw, my skin on fire as he groaned from the blow. But as I looked up through the screen door and locked eyes with her stepfather, I knew I hadn't ended a fight, but started a war.

"What the hell is going on?"

I stumbled down the steps and trudged across their yard, wiping blood from my hands down the front of my white cotton t-shirt in a daze.

"Where the hell do you think you're going," he yelled after me as the screen door squeaked open on its hinges. "I'm calling the police, you son of a bitch. I'm having you thrown in jail!"

I'd lost count of the blows as the man struggled to protect his face with his arms. "Please stop," the woman whimpered and it dawned on me her fear was no longer for the man. It was me who was making her voice quiver. I stood over his body, struggling to catch my breath as I looked over the carnage I had caused. My hands were covered in blood and I wasn't sure how much of it was my own. I couldn't feel any pain. I glanced over at the girl, concealed by the shadow of the building next to her.

"He can't hurt you now," I huffed as I stepped over him and turned toward her. She held up her hands and I stopped. Glancing back over my shoulder at him. "It's not what it looks like." I held my hand out in front of me to show her I wasn't a threat, but she continued walking backwards until her body was pressed against the brick exterior of the building.

"It looks like you just killed him." Her voice wavered in an unnaturally high pitch.

"Alright." I shook my head and ran my hand roughly through my hair. "It's exactly what it looks like." I took a tentative step forward and she pressed her body harder against the brick as a quiet whimper escaped her lips. I narrowed my eyes as I struggled to make out her features in the dim lighting. "He's not dead… unfortunately." A low moan confirmed what I had said.

"Don't come any closer. I have a gun in my purse." She clutched the bag against her chest and I let out a small laugh.

"No offense, but you lie for shit."

"I won't tell anyone." She sounded so small and fragile.

"I believe you," I took another step closer. "I'm trying to help you." I could begin to see her frightened face as my eyes adjusted. Her skin smooth and pale like cream, her eyes big and wide with fright.

"I'm not lying. I swear." Her long brown hair swayed as she shook her head and my heart froze fractionally at her resemblance to Katie. This entire situation was too eerily familiar to ignore. My gut twisted as I descended deeper into my perpetual purgatory. She was the physical manifestation of an obsession I've been unable to shake.

"What's your name?" I tried to soften my tone, afraid that if I spoke too loudly she would evaporate like the figment of my imagination that haunted me. If we didn't leave this place soon, witnesses were going to turn up but I couldn't walk away. Not this time. I'd acted on impulse and I had no idea how I was going to clean up this mess. That was the downfall of living on the road. The only people I could trust were my bandmates. I damn sure didn't trust anyone here.

Her eyes darted back and forth as she struggled to come up with something.

"What's a girl like you doing in a dark alley at this time of night anyway?" I cocked my head to the side as she sighed, her eyes going to the gravely road under her feet. I used her distraction to close the gap between us. Her eyes snapped up to mine as she tightened her grip on her bag. I searched her face, curious as to why she wasn't screaming for help or why she didn't run away while we were fighting. Her words didn't match her actions. I knew I should at least feign concern for the guy I nearly beat to death to show her I wasn't a bad guy, but I felt no remorse. My mind was only focused on her.

Slowly, I raised my hand to brush a dark lock of hair from her forehead and she flinched to prove to myself that she was really here. Her nose was a narrower and she was an inch or two taller than Katie, but my heart still stuttered. "My fingers are dirty," I mumbled as she looked at me quizzically. Her breathing hitched but she stood frozen in place, wincing as my fingertips brushed over a now exposed fresh scrape. "He do this to you?" I clenched my jaw, fighting the urge to finish what I had started. Had I not let Bryce live maybe it would really be Katie in front of me today.

She swallowed hard, breaking eye contact. "Doesn't matter," her voice thick with sadness as she shook her hair back over the wound. "I would have done worse if you hadn't butted in. I should go," she said with a shrug as her arms wrapped around her waist.

I tried not to laugh at her spitfire attitude and her equal lack of sympathy.

"I think you're in shock."

"I'm fine," her voice was void of emotion but her face looked terrified. "Nothing shocks me anymore."

"Damn it. Let me help you. Drop the fucking tough guy act."

Her body froze, aside from a slight tremor. I took a deep breath as I struggled to calm down.

I bit back my frustration. "Let me help you. I can… call someone."

Sad green eyes met mine and my chest tightened. I watched as her expression go from confusion to appreciation, she had slipped a mask in place, one very much like the one I wore daily.

"You already have," she glanced towards the man on the ground. "Th-thank you. You've done enough." With that she began walking towards the main road, her heeled-sandals against gravel the only sound I could hear over my own hammering heart. It was like a painful flashback into my past but the pain felt better than the emptiness that proceeded this moment. If it weren't for the adrenaline rush from a good fight, I'd scarcely know I was alive.

I needed to get the fuck out of there but I couldn't walk away. I had done that before and it destroyed my life. At least that's the reasoning I told myself as I jogged after her and grabbed her arm lightly. She pulled free, flinching as if she thought she was going to be hit. I took a step back immediately. "Don't go."

"I swear I won't tell anyone. I promise. I can take care of myself." Her words ran together and it dawned on me that she thought I was worried about leaving a witness or maybe it just seemed that way because it was a real concern.

"Christ, I'm not going to hurt you and if you could take care of yourself I wouldn't have had to save you back there." It was a low blow for a girl so prideful but I liked the look of fire in her eyes.

"Save me?" She glanced towards the man and back at me. "I'm not the one who needs saving."

"The world would be better off without him. Who is he? A boyfriend? Your pimp?" I asked as I looked to her hands that still held my shirt, clutched against her chest.

Her fingers trembling. There was no wedding ring and she looked like she was just barely legal. When my eyes met hers again they were narrowed and she looked like she was ready to kick my ass. It would have been cute had I not just put myself on the line for her, but I couldn't hide my smirk.

"No, he wasn't my pimp," She spat angrily, "I guess I should consider myself lucky you chose this alley for your drug deals but I think it's time for you to go back to your glass house." Her eyes were wide with anger. "Ride away on your snake, Morrison."

I held back a laugh at her Doors reference and her awkward attempt to insult me. "That wasn't," my voice trailed off as I searched for a way to explain myself but words failed me. "I wasn't trying to offend you and what you saw isn't what it looks like."

"I'd love to hear you talk your way out of all of that but I don't want to be here when he wakes up."

"He's not waking up anytime soon and he won't touch you. I won't let him."

"Thank you, my *junkie savior*, but this *hooker* has some place she needs to be."

I sighed, my tongue running over the cut inside my lip. "Can I walk you to your corner?"

Her murderous glare made me laugh as she turned and stormed off down the alley, stumbling in her heeled sandals but recovering quickly.

I began walking in the same direction and soon was at her side as she stopped to adjust her shoe.

"Stalking me now?"

"Someone's conceited." I ran my fingers over my hair. "I was actually going this way."

"Oh really? Have another batch of meth to score?" She glared at me but I saw her eyes glance down over my chest.

"Hostility is not a very attractive quality."

"Neither is sexual harassment." She began to walk faster but I stayed only a step behind.

"If I was sexually harassing you, you'd know it."

"You're a regular Prince fucking Charming. This may be hard to believe, but I don't care what you think of me."

"If you didn't care, why're you so upset?" The sound of a car approaching as the headlights bounced of the brick exterior stopped our conversation. I grabbed her wrist and began pulling her between set of apartment buildings. Our steps quickened and soon we were jogging as I tried to get my bearings. The last thing I needed was to get arrested in Orlando. We slowed to normal pace as we reached the next street over. I took my shirt from her hands and pulled it over my head, grimacing as blood from my hand smeared on to the collar. My fingers wrapped around her wrist and she didn't struggle to free herself from my grip.

CHAPTER SEVEN

ELLA
ANXIETY

**Anxiety: desire to do something,
typically accompanied by unease.**

My pulse was racing under his fingertips as we walked
the perimeter of the building and I was embarrassed that
it wasn't because of what had just happened but because
of how painstakingly handsome he was. His hair was light
brown and short but messy, and his blue eyes stood out
against his lightly tanned skin and his body was ridiculously toned. He didn't look like the man you'd picture
beating someone into unconsciousness. But I'd learned a
long time ago that the most innocent looking men can be
the most vicious. Some of the prettiest people do the ugliest
things. No one had a closet with a few skeletons in it.

"This is where I work. You can stop following me
now." I continued along the left side of the building to
the employee entrance. As I did his free hand grabbed
the door and held it open. My eyes met his again and
my knees threatened to give out as the pad of his thumb
swept over my hand.

"Try to stay out of dark alleys. You never know who is lurking in the shadows."

I tucked my hair behind my ear as his fingers slid from my wrist. "I'll do that," I mumbled as I stepped inside and the door closed between us.

I walked down the long corridor and into the small prep kitchen used to make appetizers and housed the walk-in freezer.

"You're late… again," Maric's voice stopped me in my path and I squeezed my eyes closed as I cursed myself under my breath.

"I'm sorry. There was a guy in the alley who tried to get handsy with me."

He rolled his eyes and my excuse died in my throat. You could only cry wolf so many times before people stopped listening.

"It won't happen again."

"Good. Tonight you can help with the bar and whatever the band needs. The singer is a personal friend of mine so I expect you to treat him well."

As he spoke the door to the bar opened and in walked the crazy bastard who saved my ass in the alley.

"Speak of the devil." Maric's eyes lit up as he pulled the man in for a quick hug.

"Devil? I prefer God."

"Jesus Christ, what the hell happened to you?"

"What can I say? I like it rough." He winked and my knees threatened to give out. I rolled my eyes as I fought against an audible gagging sound.

"Ella, this is Rellik."

I struggled to keep from glaring at him.

"Ella," Rellik said my name as if it were a sin, his lips curled in a devilish smirk as he held out his hand.

"Rellik, as in the guy playing here tonight?" I grinded my teeth as I placed my hand in his, the pad of his index finger sweeping over my wrist and causing my cheeks to heat.

"You're a fan?"

"God no." Pulling my hand from his, I crossed my arms over my chest.

"Ella is going to be taking care of you so if you need anything at all, don't hesitate to ask." Maric patted Rellik on the shoulder and pushed open the swinging door to the bar. "Ella," his expression turning serious as he glanced back to me. "Play nice." With that he disappeared and I was left with the man I tried so desperately to ditch only moments before.

"I love a good plot twist," Rellik's grin widened.

"I didn't really like this job anyway." I shrugged as I began walking back the long corridor, Rellik at my side. I wanted to scream and flip out. Most of all I wanted to wipe the cocky smirk off of Rellik's ridiculously sexy face. Even with a busted lip he was fucking beautiful like a cracked marble statue of a Greek god. Guys like him thought the world turned for them. I hated men like him.

"Why did you help me?" It didn't make sense for him to risk his freedom over me.

"Because you couldn't help yourself."

"No offense but you don't seem like the good Samaritan type."

He nodded to one of our security guy as we turned right down another hallway. "I'm not."

I rolled my eyes. "At least you're honest."

"That makes one of us." His hand went to the small of my back to urge me through the doorway before him and goose bumps followed in the wake of his fingertips. "I think you'll enjoy the show."

"Not a big fan of rock music."

"That so?" He grinned and I could tell I was annoying him. But that didn't stop me from rambling on further. Someone needed to knock this guy down a peg or two.

"It's just loud noise and mindless screaming."

"I can see why you have a job working with the public. So pleasant."

"I get that a lot." I tucked my long, dark hair behind my ear as we made our way down the mint colored corridor. A few people lingered in the hall and they all smiled and nodded to him and he returned the gesture as he urged me forward.

"Stay, while we rehearse. Maybe you'll change your mind," he said simply as a man in thick rimmed glasses opened a door and stepped back to let us through as I eyed the handle.

"I really can't. I have a lot of work to do."

"I could always tell Maric that you didn't want to help out."

"You're an asshole."

"I get that a lot." He mocked me as we entered another hall and continued further down, the sound of a guitar off in the distance played a slow, haunting tune that gave me chills. "That's Hangman. He can't pay attention enough to order a damn meal, but you put an instrument in his hands and he's genius." Rellik smiled over at me, his lower lip was swollen and tinged red. He must have seen my worried expression because his tongue ran over his lip. "It doesn't hurt." He reached out to open a door and the dried blood on his knuckles caused me to gasp but blood and gaping wounds was nothing new to me. Someone receiving them to defend me was what was shocking and I had been nothing but a bitch to him.

"I should clean that for you," I said and the corner of his mouth quirked into a smile as he pushed the door open. A man sat across the room on a couch with a guitar on his lap and a cigarette between his lips. His eyes were closed as he exhaled, cloaking himself in a thick haze of smoke. His fingers moved effortlessly over the strings and I was in awe of his talent.

He had strong, angular features and his hair was the color of sand with strands of honey throughout that hung haphazardly over his eyes. I inhaled and realized that what he was smoking was anything but tobacco.

"Hang, this is Ella." Rellik called out and the guy's red-rimmed eyes shot open, and he smiled. His fingers stopped and he took the joint from his mouth, relaxing back on the couch.

"You took the time to learn her name. I'm impressed."

"She's not a groupie, asshole. In fact, she hates our kind of music." Rellik replied, his voice laced with amusement.

"Is that right?" The corner of his mouth curled up in a smile as he shook his head. "A challenge."

"Where's Phantom and Trigger?" As he spoke my eyes darted around the room but it was only the three of us behind a flimsy pressed-wood door.

"Ran to get munchies from the gas station," He put the joint to his mouth and inhaled as he eyed me curiously while I tried not to stare at the large tribal tattoo that crept over his right shoulder and down his toned chest. He was in shape without an ounce of fat, but not as muscular as Rellik. "You wanna hit this?" He asked with a smile and I struggled not to roll my eyes at the double entendre. He waved the joint in the air towards me as he exhaled. "It's medicinal, I swear. It's the only way I can put up with Rellik." He winked and I felt my cheeks blush. "Something tells me you might need it."

"Make yourself at home. It might help you relax," Rellik stepped around me and walked to another guitar that was propped against the far wall. He picked it up by the neck and sat down on an oversized chair. I stood next to the door awkwardly as Hangman's eyes narrowed, scrutinizing me. It probably wasn't often a women was standoffish with them.

Rellik strummed the acoustic guitar as he began to sing, low and gravely. His eyebrows pulled together as if in pain as he continued. I forced myself to relax as I began to walk towards him. The anguish and torture in his voice spoke to me and it was like he had unraveled all of my secrets and strung them together, set to a slow steady beat that kept in time with my pulse. It wasn't anything like I expected from him after seeing how violent he could become just moments before. He was at peace and it was fascinating.

Fighting away your fears, screams falling on deaf ears. Heaven help what we've become.

**Trampled and crushed dreams, nothing was what it seems.
Our world has come undone.**

Hangman slid over to make room for me on the long couch and I sat down, keeping my distance from him and a clear view of the door. He held out the joint again and I reluctantly took it, nearly letting it slip through my shaky fingers. I looked to Rellik as I put it to my lips, sputtering and coughing as soon as the smoke filled my lungs. It felt like my chest was gripped in a vice and I struggled, desperate for fresh air. I'd smoked weed before but what I got was lawn clippings compared to this.

"Woah," Rellik grabbed a bottle of water from the stand beside the couch and held it out for me. I took it gratefully and guzzled it down. He continued playing, his voice like liquid honey, and my head began to swim as I handed the joint back to Hangman.

"So what's your story?"

**Baby, just let me in, I can wash away our sins.
I know no other way.**

I looked to Rellik who was watching me as he sang and I had no idea what to say. It was a loaded question that was impossible to answer because I didn't have an identity anymore.

"I'm a blank page."

"Deep," Phantom took another hit from the joint.

"So why do they call you Hangman?"

He raised his chin to the light so I could see the very faded scar that circled his neck. "Fucking intense, right?" He laughed and I tried to keep the shock from my face.

The music stopped abruptly as two men entered and I was glad for the end to the odd conversation.

"Look who decided to show," the larger of the two said. He was well over six foot tall and he must have worked out obsessively. A thick black paint stripe, that matched his short hair, ran down the length of his face just beside his nose and it made him look absolutely terrifying.

"You knew I'd be back," Rellik replied blowing off the stern look from the tallest one. "Phantom, this is Ella." He motioned to me and the large man glanced in my direction, his eyes narrowing as if he knew me but couldn't place from where.

"Phantom," I smiled. "Like Phantom of the Opera!"

"Glad to see you're still in one piece." He said with no humor and I realized he must have been the other man across the alley.

"Thank you."

"*No* thanks to you," Rellik chimed in and Phantom gave him a death glare. "Not that I needed any help. The bigger they are, the harder they fall."

"I'm Trig," The other man said. His hair was much like Hangman's but brushed back so it didn't hang in his eyes and he wore a set of silver dog tags around his neck over a plain white t-shirt and all four of them wore weathered jeans. My eyebrows furrowed but I couldn't figure his name out. "As in Trigger." He grabbed his dog tags to show me he had been in the military.

"Nice to meet you," I cleared my throat before taking another drink from the water bottle. He nodded and they both looked to Rellik. "Your hands look like shit."

"You should see the guys face, but to be fair he wasn't very pretty to begin with," He glanced up at Trig with a playful grin absent of any remorse. The idea that he could brush off something like that made me envious and a little frightened.

Phantom ran his hand roughly through his short dark hair, clearly frustrated with Rellik but he didn't say anything.

"Here." Rellik dug into his pocket and pulled out a pill bottle, tossing it to Trig. "You can't just go off your meds, Trigger. You know your head gets all fucked up when you don't take them."

"What are you, my fucking mom now?" Trig asked as he shook his head, but his smile gave away that he appreciated the gesture. My eyes met Rellik's and I couldn't help but smile myself as he cocked his eyebrow.

"One ugly mother," Hangman joked, his laugh turning into a cough as he fell on his side.

"There's got to be a first aid kit around here." I was getting whiplash from Rellik's personality.

"Don't worry about it. We need to rehearse," Rellik replied and the room was silent for a minute before I pushed to my feet, water in hand and searched out something I could use to help wipe away the dried blood. He clearly wasn't accustomed to anyone taking care of him and I could understand his apprehension.

"You've come over to the dark side. Tired of the bleach smell from those other bitches?" One of them said behind me and I tried not to cringe at how they spoke as if I wasn't a person. Of course he was into dumb blondes. Did other women really tolerate this?

I grabbed some napkins and silently took a mental note of what type of females they generally hung out with, hating that my stomach sank when I looked down at my dark tresses. It was important to read people and learn everything about them as quickly as possible. It's how you survived. You blend in, not stand out. Making the napkins damp I crossed the room and knelt down in front of him. I looked up at him as I reached for his hand and he let me pull it away from the guitar. I carefully ran it over his injured and he tensed as I ran over a knuckle that was clearly swollen more than the others. The guys began to chat amongst themselves about the show and Rellik leaned closer to me as I took his other hand.

"You didn't have to do this."

"You didn't have to help me either, but you did. It's rare." I hated to admit that I had needed him there. I scrubbed as much of the blood as I could and luckily most of it wasn't his own. "That's better," I pushed to my feet and let go of his hand, his calloused fingertips sliding over mine. *He had worked hard for what he has. It wasn't handed to him.* I wadded up the napkins and tossed them in a small trash bin along the wall. The guys all settled into the couch and I sat in a folding chair along the wall as they began to go over their set list.

My brain was a fuzzy haze and none of what happened tonight seemed real. But tomorrow I would have to face the consequences of what had transpired as it would undoubtedly manifest in to nightmares and anxiety. The unease began to spread and panic settled deep in a knot in my belly and slowly spidered through my veins like poison. I began to count, whispering rapidly under my breath. I should have known better than to use drugs that only exasperate paranoia and fear.

"*One.*"

"*Two.*"

"*Three.*"

"*Four.*"

"*Five.*"

Rellik lifted the guitar from his lap and sat it on the floor beside him as he stood. "Are you alright?" He asked, his voice echoed in my mind. I stood, wobbling on my feet as I became lightheaded and panicked.

"I'm fine. I just… need some fresh air. I must have hit my head harder than I realized."

Chapter Eight

RELLIK
CATALYST

Catalyst: a person or thing that precipitates an event.

"What the fuck was in that weed, Hang?" Trigger asked as I stood in front of Ella, examining her.

"The shock is wearing off," I called over my shoulder.

"Chicks are too fucking delicate," Hangman joked, clearly he smoked away his sensitivity.

"I'm fine," she mumbled but wouldn't look me in the eye as she turned for the door. I looked back at the guys knowing if she left now she would break down and have no one to turn to. "It's just a panic attack. It's not a big deal."

"Let me take you home or something." I clenched my jaw knowing I was going to delay the concert but I couldn't just let her go.

"No. Maric will fire me."

"I can handle Maric."

"I don't need you to fight my battles for me."

"Clearly you do."

"Rellik," Phantom called out and the deep bass in his voice caused Ella to jump, her hand on her chest if trying to keep her heart from escaping. "She doesn't want your help. Let it go."

I turned to her and took a deep breath, forcing myself to bury growing anger towards him. "I'll walk you out." I stepped to her side and placed my hand on the small of her back, urging her forward and into the hall. "I'll be right back," I promised the guys with empty words. I had no choice. The look in her eye may have been from different circumstances but I'd seen it in my own reflection. I knew what it felt like to be screaming for someone, anyone to give a fuck about you.

"You know that's not what I'm worried about," Phantom said quietly as I pulled the door closed behind us.

I knew her resemblance to Katie was clouding my judgment, but I had to help her. What kind of person would I be had I left her in that alley? It wasn't about Katie. It w*asn't.*

"Thank you," she said as we walked through the mint colored labyrinth of hallways, counting her footsteps under her breath, to the back exit. As we hit the warm night air behind the parking lot I pulled one of the security aside.

"I need the car."

He nodded and spoke into his ear pierce. Ella looked like she was falling apart and I wanted to be able to comfort her, but playing the nice guy wasn't something I had a lot of experience at. I saved her and that would have to be enough. I wasn't wired any other way. Within minutes a black SUV pulled up beside us and the guard driving got out and walked around the car to open the passenger door.

"You're not listening to me. I'm not leaving. I just need some air." Something was bothering her and I wasn't sure the attack in the alley was the catalyst. This chick didn't seem like the type to cower in a corner to lick her wounds.

"Fine," I motioned to the man and the car was taken back to the employee lot. I leaned against the metal exterior of the building, the wall still holding in the heat from an unbearable day. She pressed her back against the wall next to me as I pulled a pack of cigarettes from his pocket, popping one in my mouth.

"Those will kill you," She I folded her arms over her chest, hugging herself.

"I'm touched you care." I pulled it from my mouth and flipped it over in my hand. "I haven't lit one in six months. I like knowing I can if I want to."

"So you're spoiled. Used to always getting what you want."

"No." I shook my head as I broke the cigarette in half and glanced over at her. "Not always."

"Thank you. I'm not sure I said it back there but *thank you* for helping me."

"It's not easy to admit we need help sometimes. I get it." I knew it was hard for her to say the words. She was damn near as stubborn as I was.

"But I was rude. It wasn't fair."

"Christ, I think I liked it better when you were mean. Why the change?"

"Not used to people being nice to you?"

"Not genuinely. They usually want something in return. I kind of like this whole bitchy thing you had going on." We fell silent as I thought that over. There was less guilt when she didn't like me.

"So being in a band? That's kind of crazy, huh?"

"It sounds a lot better than it is. I like what I do and I never wanted… uh… never wanted to do anything else." My eyebrows pulled together and I swallowed hard as I struggled to keep my thoughts at bay. "But it's work, like anything else. It's lonely."

"Still, must be nice to get to do what you love."

"Love." I cringed, struggling to keep a pained expression from my face, but the back door opened and Hangman stuck his head outside. "It's just a job."

"We gotta go, man." Hangman let the door slam behind him and my gaze fell to Ella.

"You okay? We can stay out here if you want."

"Why doesn't it bother you about, you know, what you did to that guy?"

"It does bother me."

"You can't tell."

"No offense, but you don't know me, Ella. Beating up some asshole for manhandling a woman doesn't rank on my list of things to give a shit about. It bothers me, but not for the reason it should." I turned back around to the door, pulling it open for her.

"I just want to make sure you're one of the good guys." She stepped inside and I followed behind her.

"I'm not." Ella's resemblance to Katie was kicking my mind into overdrive. It was like she was the blade on my veins and every second was a push against my flesh.

"You don't need to handcuff him. He's a good kid!" My mom was panicking as tears streamed down her face. "Do something!" Mr. Thomas had his arm around her as he interjected.

"I can assure you this is just a case of boys rough-housing. Let me call Bryce's parents. I'm sure we can work this out on our own."

The officer clicked the cuff in place around my left wrist and sighed with frustration. "Your son assaulted another boy, fracturing his jaw in two places and left a two inch gash in the back of his head. We take that very seriously. He could have killed him."

"He's not my dad," I snapped but when my eyes met my mother's she flinched. It wasn't enough her only son stood before her, handcuffed and covered in someone else's blood. I had insulted her on top of everything.

"What would your father think?" Her words seared through me like a scalding knife. It didn't matter. I didn't care what anyone thought as long as Katie was safe.

"What do you care, Ma? You sure as hell didn't care what he thought when you were off screwing my guidance counselor behind his back. Bryce deserved what he got. Dad didn't."

My mother's face twisted in horror. "Your father died in someone else's car." Her sobs fell on deaf ears. I never forgot that the both of them told me they ate at the same restaurant at the time of his accident.

"And now you get to live with someone else."

I watched as Ella made her way down the hallway towards the kitchen and I went back to grab my guitar before meeting the band at the stage.

The guys were pacing the floor when I returned and we were rushed onto the stage. The building was packed and the DJ had already stayed a half hour later than he was paid for.

"What the fuck are you doing?" Phantom was by my side as I walked towards the stage.

"Don't worry about me."

"I'm not." He stepped in front of me and placed his hand on my chest to stop me from continuing on. "I'm worried about the band and that girl."

"She was fucking attacked. I couldn't just leave her alone."

"You could have. You *should* have. She's not Katie."

"I fucking know that," I snapped, stepping forward until my chest hit his.

"Then leave her alone. She's safe. Walk away."

"She needed me."

"*We* need you." He shook his head, worry in his eyes. "And that girl wouldn't step anywhere near you if she knew about your past."

"Good thing no one is going to tell her."

After I'd lost Katie something inside of me had snapped and crumbled. My obsession with her was like an addict chasing his next high. But nothing compared to that first time. It would never be enough. No one was able to compare to the girl with sad eyes and dirty hair who stole my heart and took it to her grave. I wanted to claw my way to her and become suffocated by her embrace.

Shoving by Phantom I climbed the steps leading onto the stage. I adjusted the height of my mic stand in front of the crowd as some danced and mingled, while others sipped drinks from their tables. Hangman took a seat behind his drums and Phantom, our bassist stood to my right and Trigger, our main guitarist was on my left. We decided to start things off with a cover of Animal I Have Become by Three days Grace. It was a fitting song for all of the old emotions brought to the forefront tonight. I pulled my blood-stained shirt over my head and tossed it on the ground behind me as I slipped my guitar strap over my head.

As I finished the first verse, the lights flashing around us, causing the crowd to cheer. Girls swarmed the stage with plastic cups in hand. It wasn't a big venue but was one of the larger crowds that we've played to recently. My eyes sought out Ella and I found her behind the bar talking to a few patrons as she filled their drinks. I tried to ignore her, needing to clear my head. Being back in Orlando was hard enough on me. Phantom was right but it didn't matter.

So what if you can see the darkest side of me?
No one will ever change this animal I have become

The song ended and we played into our next cover by Three Days Grace song, Pain. I tapped my foot to the beat as I gripped the mic with both hands as I sang, Trigger and Hangman singing backup. I made eye contact with various women but the only one I had on my mind was Ella, which brought me back to Katie. I closed my eyes and sang through the tightening of my chest.

"My step-dad wants to sue you for medical expenses."

"Your step-dad is an asshole." I paced in front of Katie *as she stood a few feet away, illuminated by the moon that filtered through the trees. I wanted to rush over to her and*

pull her against me, but after what I had done to her step-brother, I didn't know if she wanted me to. I didn't know if her feelings for me had changed. The idea of being without her terrified me. She had helped me through the loss of my dad and if it weren't for her I'd lose my mind.

"Has Bryce fucked with you?"

"He barely says a word to me but I know he knows why you did it."

"Good. I'm glad he knows. That motherfucker better not put his hands on you again."

She sighed heavily as she walked slowly towards me, sadness in her eyes. I knew she wanted to say something about my swearing, like she always did, but she said nothing. I wanted her to scold me, to tell me she didn't like it. At least then I would know she still cared.

"What is it?"

"My step-dad called the principal and talked to Mr. Thomas. He wants to change my classes so I'm not anywhere near you." She stopped in front of me as she looked at the ground between us.

I pulled her against my chest as I stared up at the moon through the trees as my arms tightened. I hated having to sneak out to meet her. If she got caught she would get in a lot of trouble, but I couldn't stay away from her. Katie and I were meant to be together. No one was going to stop that.

"I'll talk to Mr. Thomas. He won't let that happen. I'll fix it for us."

"Bryce told them he saw you flirting with me and he told you to leave me alone and that's why you attacked him. He said he was going to tell my mom about us if I didn't

stay away from you." She pulled back from my embrace to look at me and it killed me to see her so sad.

"Katie, you have to tell them the truth. At least tell your mom. She'll understand."

"After what you did to Bryce? They wanted to press charges. They want to send me live with my dad in Charlotte. I don't want to go."

It was selfish of me to be happy she didn't want to be away from me, but I didn't trust Bryce to leave her alone. The guy was a first class asshole. The only reason anyone tolerated him was because he was the best player they had on the football team.

"I won't let that happen, Katie."

"Maybe we should just stay away from each other for a while."

"What? What are you saying?" My mind raced as I reached out for her and she folded her arms over her chest. "Katie, I would never hurt you. You know that right? Katie!"

"I know that." She took a step back and like the twig that cracked under her foot, so did my heart.

"Then why are you hurting me?"

As I reached the chorus I opened my eyes and they landed on Ella's. My tongue ran over the cut on my lip as we began to play an original song of ours.

To the untrained eye she's hanging by a thread
But she's a black widow and she's spinning a web
Hotter than sin and hell bent on pain
She'll eat you alive until nothing remains but...
LOVE will be the death of us all
LOVE until you crumble and fall
LOVE just another reason to cry

Fuck love, Fuck you, I don't want your lie
Begging for mercy and waiting to attack
The knife in your heart slides into your back
Kill or be killed but you're dying for her
Sin tasted, life wasted because there's no cure for…
LOVE will be the death of us all
LOVE until you crumble and fall
LOVE just another reason to cry
Fuck love, Fuck you, I don't want your lie

We continued the set singing a few original songs and a couple more covers before the night was over and I could finally get off stage. I needed something to calm my mind and the blonde who had just grabbed my arm and pressed her chest against mine normally would be the perfect choice. But when I glanced up again to the bar, the smile Ella had worn through the night had faded and in that fraction of a second her mask slipped.

"Give me a minute," I stepped around the woman and made my way through the crowd to the bar.

"Need a drink?" She tucked her hair behind her ear as she filled a mug of beer from the tap, but her mind was elsewhere.

"Double shot of Jack, straight up."

She smirked and shook her head. "And for your *friend*?" She glanced over my shoulder and I looked behind me to see the blonde I had just brushed off before looking back to Ella.

"*You* can pour yourself one as well, if you think you can handle it."

Her smile broadened as I blew off the other woman. She poured out our drinks and sat my glass in front of me, raising her own towards her lips. "Challenge accepted. What are we drinking to?"

I grabbed my own glass, spinning it in my fingers as the amber liquid sloshed against the side of the cup. "To dark alleys." I drank back the shot, letting it burn down my throat without a chaser.

"To dark alleys." She drank slowly, her eyebrows furrowed like she was in pain but she didn't stop as I struggled not to laugh.

"Are you going to hang out for the after party?" I asked as she took my glass and poured again.

"Actually, when my shift ends I have something I have to do."

"What's that?" I asked and she tilted her head to the side. "A date?"

"You ask a lot of questions about things that aren't any of your business." She poured herself a single and drank it down a little quicker than the last, scrunching up her nose at the taste.

"You don't have to pretend you like whiskey just to prove something to me."

"I'm not." She tried her best to hide the disgust from her face.

"You don't have to pretend you don't like *me*."

She leaned forward resting her elbows on the bar to get closer. "Is it really that hard for you to believe not *everyone* wants to fuck you?"

I closed the gap between us and her gaze dropped to my lips. "No one said anything about fucking, sweetheart." I cocked my head to the side as embarrassment washed over her, tinting her cheeks a sexy shade of pink.

CHAPTER NINE

ELLA
SWOON

Swoon: Faint from extreme emotion.

His cockiness was getting under my skin. Watching all of the women swoon over him as he sang, I could see why it was so easy to react to him that way. But I had way too much on my mind to fall for bedroom eyes.

"Let me take you home."

I coughed, shocked at his brazen words. "Excuse me?" He was still shirtless in front of me and my eyes drifted down over his bare, toned chest.

"So you don't have to walk in the alley. I want to make sure you make it home safe. Is *everything* about sex with you, Ella?"

I felt my face heat from misunderstanding him and I wanted to slap the smirk from his lips. Maybe my mind was in the gutter. I shook my head as I ran a damp rag over the bar. "Yeah, rumor has it some lunatic beat the hell out of some guy earlier tonight." I pictured the eviction notice on my door. I had no idea where I was going to go tonight but I had suffered enough humiliation for one day and was desperate to change the subject.

"Why do the other guys go by nicknames and you don't? Not very creative."

"What the hell does *that* mean?"

"I dunno," she chewed her lip as she fought against a smile. "The other guys have these scary names and yours kind of sounds like a third generation tea kettle on the Antique Road Show. Not something that evokes fear."

He laughed loudly as he shook his head. "Relic. Never thought of it that way."

Rellik smiled crookedly as he leaned over the bar, snatching a pen from my apron. Grabbing a beer coaster he wrote out his name in capital letters before sliding it to me.

"I don't get it."

"Turn around. Look in the mirror behind the bar."

I spun around as I held it up to my chest, glancing between the rows of liquor bottles. "Killer," I mumbled.

"Hiding in plain sight. What's more dangerous than that?" His blue eyes were alive with amusement.

Phantom walked up behind Rellik, his eyes narrowed as he stared me down. "Here," he shoved Rellik's shirt into his chest forcefully. Rellik's expression turned dark like it had been in the alley. "We have some people in the back waiting to meet you. Blonde, just like you like." His eyes landed on mine again making sure I understood he meant women before turning and walking into the crowd. I got the hint that I wasn't welcome back there anymore, even if it was my job to make sure they were taken care of.

"So, um…" I tucked my hair behind my ear as I looked around for what to do next. "I still have another hour. I should get back to work." I hurried down the bar to refill a beer. I didn't glance back at Rellik's seat as I tended to my other customers. When I finally did glance back in his direction, he was gone and someone else was in his spot. I was relieved and disappointed.

The crowd was steady for the next hour and when I finally was able to cash out, my feet were killing me and Mandy took over the bar until closing. But even with the extra hours I had barely made enough with tips to feed myself, let alone get a room for the night.

I grabbed my book bag that held a few items of clothing and slung it over my shoulder as I stepped into the kitchen. "I'm off," I told Maric with a wave. He nodded his head, not bothering to turn around. The mint corridor had a few lingering patrons who had spilled out from the band's party. I shook my head as I sidestepped my way around them and shoved open the back door. The night air was muggy and as the door closed behind me I jumped as I noticed Rellik leaning up against the wall, an unlit cigarette in his hand.

I pulled my bag up on my shoulder and nodded to him as I began to walk along the building. I could hear his footsteps close behind me on the gravel.

"What are you doing?"

"Walking you home."

I groaned as I bit down on my lower lip. "I told you I didn't need you to walk me home."

"I'm not asking your permission."

"Phantom won't be happy." I rolled my eyes as he pulled a lighter from his pocket and lit the cigarette in his hand.

"I didn't ask his permission either." He took a deep pull, inhaling the smoke into his lungs before expelling the cloud around him. His mood seemed to have considerably changed from the bar and I wanted to ask him what had happened but it wasn't my place. "I thought you quit."

He looked down at the cigarette in his hand as we continued to walk but he didn't respond. "So what is his problem anyway? He doesn't seem to like me very much." I glanced to the spot that the man had attacked me earlier, clutching my purse to my side.

"It's not you." He shook his head but didn't elaborate.

"The thing about conversations, Rellik, is they usually go two ways."

He flicked the cigarette onto the ground and orange embers scattered as it hit. "He's pissed at me, not you."

"It's touching he has such an active interest in your personal life. Afraid it will taint your reputation to be seen talking to a brunette?" My attempt at a joke fell on deaf ears.

His eyes met mine and he swallowed hard like he wanted to say something but didn't.

"Well, I appreciate you looking after me. This is me." I pointed to the apartment building behind me.

"I'll walk you up."

"You don't have to do that."

His eyes narrowed like he could see through my words and his hand ran over the stubble of his jaw. "Let's just pretend we argued about it and I decided I was going to walk you up anyway. Save us both some time."

I groaned, my shoulders sagging under the impending embarrassment. "Well, I can save us even more time and tell you I sort of got evicted today."

"What?"

"I got kicked out," he cut me off as I spoke.

"I know what evicted means, Ella. Why didn't you tell me? What were you going to do? Sleep in the stairwell?"

"And what would telling you accomplish? Embarrassment added to my already shitty day? I can take care of myself."

He laughed sardonically as he shook his head and looked to the ground between us, his hand running over the back of his hair. "Clearly. Come on." His long fingers looped around my wrist and I hated how deprived I've been of human contact that it made my heart race. Maybe that was just a side effect of Rellik. He pulled me back up the alley towards the bar and I struggled to keep pace with him. He wasn't giving me a chance to argue and I was grateful because I really had no idea what I was going to do.

Chapter Ten

RELLIK
PLACATE

Placate: to soothe or mollify especially by concessions.

When we reached the bar Ella began pulling back from my grip.

"What?" I asked as I looked around.

"I don't want to make things worse for you and the other guys. It would be really shitty for me to cause any more problems with you guys."

"Phantom is my problem, not yours. You didn't do anything wrong."

"What about..." She began to chew the side of her lip and I couldn't help but laugh as I motioned to the security to bring our car around.

"I'm taking you to a hotel. I won't subject you to the acts of depravity that go on after a gig."

"Oh." She tucked her hair behind her ears and stared off into the parking lot. The security pulled up with my SUV. He got out and ran to the passenger side, pulling the door open.

"Thanks," I patted him on the shoulder and he nodded as he stepped back. I motioned for Ella to climb in and she did without a word. "I'll just be a few minutes," I called out to the bouncer as I walked around the front of the vehicle.

As I slid into the driver seat, Ella staring blankly out of the front window. She no longer looked upset over losing her apartment. She sat expressionless and somehow that was worse because I couldn't see what she was dealing with.

I shifted into drive and drove across the lot. Accelerating more than necessary, I turned onto the main road lined with motels but there was no vacancy. The silence was uncomfortable but I only made things worse when I opened my mouth.

"I'm not sure what you need me to do here, Ella. Tell me what to do." She didn't respond. "Does your head hurt?" I glanced toward her but couldn't see the tiny scrape that was concealed by her hair.

She shook her head and her hand went up to rub over the scrape under her long, side-swept bangs.

"I can take you to a doctor or something." I knew the mark was superficial, but I felt like I was doing the wrong thing at every step.

"I'm fine. I'm tougher than I look."

I travelled a few miles down the road, pulling off into a Marriot. "This uhh… this is where my room is," I said as I put the vehicle into park. Her seat belt unclicked and she squeezed the handle on the door causing it to pop open.

"Thank you," she said as she began to step out.

I reached into my pocket, stretching my leg out when I remembered I had given my cash to Phantom. "Shit," I shook my head and looked over at her as she worried her lip.

"It's fine, really. You've done enough. I'll find somewhere to go." She stepped out of the car and I got out as well and jogged around to her side.

I slid my hand into my back pocket and pulled out a plastic key card, and held it out for her. Her eyes narrowed as she looked it over. "You can stay in my room."

"No," she laughed nervously and waved her hands.

"Do you want to go back to the after party?" I quirked an eyebrow as my eyes travelled down her body. "You might enjoy it."

"I really just want to sleep and forget this day ever happened."

"I'll get another room when I get back. It's not a big deal." I tried not to take her words personally.

Her eyes locked on to mine, before she slowly nodded, still unsure but deciding against arguing.

I began walking across the dark lot toward the rooms as she followed close behind. I pulled a keycard from my pocket and slid it into the card reader.

I shook my head as she glanced over at me as she slowly stepped inside and I reached in to turn on the light. It wasn't a large room but I didn't plan on spending much time in it while I was here.

She walked around the room, folding her arms over her chest. "It's nice," she said quietly. "For some reason I expected strippers and a disco ball."

I laughed, "My room is the only time I get to be alone."

"Oh," she mumbled as she looked around the space again. I knew she must have been thinking about the after party. As much as she pretended she wasn't attracted to me I could tell she was, just like I was pulled to her.

"Are you going to be okay?" I slid the card into my back pocket as she sank down on the edge of the double bed, an awkwardness settling between us at the fact I was heading to that very place now sank in.

"Yeah. I'll be fine." She gave me a small smile and I nodded, not sure what else to say.

"If you need anything," I grabbed the hotel pen from the side table and jotted down my cell phone number on the stationary. "You can call. These things can run kinda late but I'll be back before dawn. I'll check on you." I handed her the paper and she folded it in half, sliding it into the back pocket of her jeans as I walked towards the door.

"I enjoyed your show."

"Thanks. The crowd seemed to like our loud noise and mindless screaming," I joked as I pulled the door open to leave.

"You're really good, Ryder."

"What?" I turned back to face Ella as she rain her fingers through the tangles in her hair. I hadn't been called Ryder for years, not after I finally left this place.

"You're a really good *writer*. Those lyrics you sang felt so… personal. Maybe rock music isn't so bad." She smiled, dimples settling in her cheeks, oblivious to what I thought I heard twisted my stomach.

I nodded as I looked her over, but my head was swimming. "Maybe you will get to see us perform again some other time." She wouldn't. Phantom was right.

"That'd be nice."

I pulled the door closed behind me and breathed in the night air, my chest feeling constricted.

I didn't remember the ride back to the bar as I struggled against the demons inside of my head, pulling me under, watching me slip back into the darkness I used to surround myself in.

I could hear them whispering around me, pointing and snickering about what I had done to Bryce.

"I heard he tried to kill him and coach had to beat his ass on their front lawn," David from third period Algebra whispered from behind me in class. He was another worthless jock and close friend of Bryce.

"He doesn't look like he got his ass beat," Erin replied as he laughed. "But my dad said when they arrested Ryder, Mr. Thomas was at his house. He's screwing Ryder's mom! No wonder they let him come back to school."

"He was covered in Bryce's blood! He was just trying to protect his sister. Ryder attacked her for no reason."

I glanced down at the steering wheel to my cut and bruised knuckles, flexing my grip as I cracked my neck. I needed to quiet the voices but with Ella everything was bubbling to the surface.

"I bet when he's a serial killer they'll call him Red Ryder," Erin's laugh nearly sent me over the edge but I had to stay out of trouble.

I didn't care if they thought I was crazy as long as I got to see Katie, but the day was nearly over and I hadn't crossed her path once. I was beginning to worry that on top of her schedule change she really was avoiding me. I couldn't stop the nagging voice inside my head from telling me I'd lost her, that I wouldn't be able to keep her safe. After I'd snuck out to meet her my mother took my phone and any means of communication. I knew she felt like she was helping me but it just made me feel even more alone. School was my only chance of seeing Katie. If it weren't for her I wouldn't have even shown up today. I tapped my pencil against my desk as my leg moved with the same unspent energy that was building inside of me. Three long days since I met her in the woods. Three days since I was able to hold her in my arms and promise her I'd protect her. Three days since she ripped my heart from my chest and left me alone, broken and bleeding.

"Maybe he killed his dad," David's voice pierced my thoughts and without thinking I shoved my desk, sending it toppling on its side as I stood. Still healing wounds on my knuckles split as my fist connected with his temple, sending him falling from his chair, his head bouncing from the old tile floor with a sickening thud.

"Maybe I should kill you," I swung again, leaning over his chair as he lay curled in a fetal position on the floor. My fist struck his arm as he covered his face.

"Ryder," Mr. Jones yelled over the crowd of screaming girls and a handful of guys who called for David to beat my ass. The teacher's arms banded around my chest from behind and I didn't struggle as I tried to calm my rapid breathing. My eyes danced over my fellow classmates, wide-eyed and in shock from my outburst. It was one thing to hear the rumors of what they think I had done,

but to see me react so violently only solidified my craziness in their minds.

I'd reacted without thinking, given them what they needed to make my life a living hell.

"Call the office!"

It didn't take long for Mr. Thomas to race to my classroom, the look of disappointment on his face letting me know how bad I'd fucked up. I'd been counting down the days for him to be transferred to his new job, hating that he had so effortlessly stepped into my father's shoes and intertwined himself into every aspect of my life. But I knew that if he weren't the one standing before me in this moment, I'd be in the back of a cop car again.

"It's okay," he held out his hand and slowly Mr. Jones released his grip on me. I shrugged free, taking one last glance around the room before storming off past Mr. Thomas and out of the classroom door.

He was quick on my heels as I stomped down the hall angrily. "Where is she? Why haven't I seen her all day?"

"Ryder, you can't keep acting like this. I can't help you anymore. Your mother is going to lose her mind when she finds out what you just did."

I stopped and turned to face him, causing him to stop suddenly to avoid running into me. "Then don't tell her." At sixteen I was only an inch taller than him and I could see hesitation in his eyes. He was like them. He believed I was some kind of monster and I was dangerously close to falling over the edge.

"I can't keep secrets from your mother." He shook his head but I could see the lack of confidence in his stance. He was lying. But I didn't have time to worry about his problems.

I lowered my voice, begging for someone to see reason. "I would never hurt Katie. I would never do the things they are saying I tried to do to her. I was protecting her from Bryce."

"I know that. I know." He nodded but I knew he was placating me, hoping to defuse the situation. He wasn't hearing anything I was saying and it was infuriating.

"Then why are you looking at me like they do? Why won't you tell me where she is so I can see that she's okay?"

"Come to my office and I can explain." His voice was too calm and I wanted to scream at him, to make him understand how serious this was.

"Explain it now," My jaw was clenched in anger and I knew I was getting louder. It wouldn't be long until a teacher became curious and stuck their head out in the hall.

He sighed, his shoulders dropping fractionally as he rubbed his fingers over his forehead, as if to force the right answer to appear. "Her mother signed her out of school this morning. She's moving to her father's in North Carolina. She's safe. You don't need to worry about her."

"Why didn't you tell me? How could you not tell me? You can't let them do this. I need to see her."

"I don't have a choice and honestly, I think it might be for the best. You're too wrapped up in her. At your age you should be going on dates with different girls and hanging out with friends. Had I known about the two of you sooner, I would have intervened. You got arrested, Ryder. You brought the cops to your mother's door. That can't happen again."

"No. You don't understand. She's not just some girl. Katie was there for me when I had no one."

"You have your mother. You have me. After you father died," His voice died as I lurched toward him.

"No!" I was in his face, my breathing coming so rapidly my chest was pressed against his. "You don't get to talk about my dad. You don't get to say shit. You barely waited until his body was cold before you were all over my mom."

"That's not fair, Ryder. You're projecting your anger onto me."

"If I was, you'd fucking know it. I have to see her before she goes." I turned to walk away, no plan in mind. I just needed to tell Katie that I'd wait for her or I'd run with her.

Mr. Thomas grabbed my arm and I spun around causing him to flinch as if I'd hit him. "Think things through, Ryder. You're only going to cause her more trouble, cause all of us more trouble. This is what is best for Katie."

"I'm what's best for Katie. I was only trying to protect her and you left me with no way to talk to her, to make sure she was safe. She wouldn't leave without saying goodbye." I ran my fingers through my hair, gripping it and pulling, adrenaline causing me to shake with anger. I couldn't get my thoughts in order. Katie had always been the voice of reason, the only thing that could stop my mind from racing.

Mr. Thomas put his hand on my shoulder, pity in his expression. "First love is the hardest to get over. If you just give it some time."

I knocked his hand away and he took a step back. "I'm not going to get over Katie."

I stormed off down the hall and out the front door of the school, pacing the sidewalk as I waited for the cops to arrive.

CHAPTER ELEVEN

ELLA
SURVIVOR

Survivor: to continue to function or prosper.

The room was small but clean and the hotel had been recently built so it didn't feel seedy and dirty. The walls were white and the bed and accent furniture a deep blue that reminded me of Rellik's eyes. There was a bed in the center with a dresser directly in front of it that held a flat screen television. I turned it on to have some background noise so it didn't feel so empty. I hated being alone ever since I was little.

On the far side was small desk and chair that shared a wall with the bathroom. On top of the desk was a black duffle bag. I stepped inside the bathroom and flipped on the light. The walls and floor were covered in tiny one inch tiles all different shades of blue. The shower had a thick glass door that made the room appear larger. A sink that looked like a glass bowl on a beautiful reclaimed wood table was to the right next to the toilet. It was very modern and streamline and I was dying to take a hot shower and wash away the stress of the day. I looked up at the mirror and took in my dark circles under my eyes. My hair desperately needed a trim and a few hours in the sun would do my skin some good.

I turned on the shower, giving it time to get warm as I took of my clothes and tossed them in a pile by the sink. I grabbed the soap bar from the shelf and ripped open the plastic wrapping. Rubbing it between my wet hands I glanced down the fading scars on my torso and thighs. I tried not to think about how they had gotten there. I wore them as a badge of honor because each mark was another tally in the list of things I'd survived.

"Stop pretending you don't like me." He took a long drink from a beer bottle and sat it on the bathroom sink. I covered myself, trying to hide behind the spray of the shower to obscure his view.

"Get out of here."

"Make me."

"You don't scare me!" I knew my lip was quivering and I took a step back as he grabbed a razor from the sink, a sadistic smirk on his face.

"You look scared, Mikaella." He stepped toward me as I slipped, falling in the tub. Laughing he bent down over me and ran the blade against my upper thigh, leaving behind a one inch gash. I screamed as the pain seared through me, but there was no one else home, no one to come save me.

"I love it when you scream." He grabbed himself over his jeans as I pushed myself to my feet, refusing to let him have his way.

"I'll tell them! I don't care if they send me back!"

"Tell them what? That you cut yourself shaving? Maybe they'll send you to psych ward. Does that sound fun?" he

grabbed my wrist with so much force it felt like the bones would crumble beneath my bruised flesh.

"When my father finds me he is going to kill you," I seethed.

"Oh, that's cute. You think your real parents are going to come for you? Why don't we have a little more fun until they arrive?"

Stepping under the spray I closed my eyes and cleaned myself as quickly as possible, a habit I had developed over the last few years. The flesh over my right hip was tender from the alley fight and I exhaled through clenched teeth as I rubbed over it again and again until the pain no longer caused me to wince. They couldn't hurt me anymore. No one could hurt me.

I quickly lathered up my hair with the complimentary mini shampoo bottle and rinsed away the smell of sweat and stale beer. I splayed my fingers out in front of me and watched my hand tremor. It had been years since I had slept without the aid of his medicine and tonight was going to be brutal.

I grabbed the small, rough white towel that hung just outside of the shower door and tried to wrap my body, but even with my small frame I was unable to get it around me. I padded out the bed leaving wet footprints behind me and glanced around the room. I couldn't put my dirty clothes back on until I washed them and they would be uncomfortable to sleep in.

I glanced over at the door as I slowly unzipped the duffle bag. It was full of men's clothing, a journal and a few odds and ends. I grabbed a gray Doors t-shirt and a pair of grey boxers that would pass as shorts while I looked for the laundry mat in the hotel. I pulled the clothes on quickly and a small folded piece of notebook paper caught my eye. I pulled it out of the bag and unfolded it. It had a phone number with no name. I stuck it back inside the bag and grabbed a blue bottle of cologne, Polo Sport. Pulling off the silver lid I sniffed it before spritzing some of it on the t-shirt before dropping it bag inside. Under the clothing was an old notebook, I glanced to the door as I pulled it out and flipped it open to a random page. Random lyrics were scribbled across the pages in different colored ink. Some looked much newer than others.

Dark and dirty, your secrets untold
You should have been mine to have and to hold
Blood on my hands, emptiness in my heart
Time came too soon for death do us part

I shoved the notebook back under the clothing as I thought over the lyrics. Zipping the bag closed, I pulled the collar of shirt to my nose and breathed in the scent again. It was masculine and clean and I could have bathed in that scent. I rounded the bed and rung my hands together as I looked at the hotel phone.

I gripped the receiver and took a deep breath as I lifted it from its base and dialed the only phone number I still had committed to memory. After three rings a deep voice answered.

"Hello?" With that one word my heart sank and my stomach twisted in pain. He spoke again but it was the female's voice in the background that caught my attention. I wrapped the cord around my finger but didn't respond. "Mikaella," he whispered into the receiver.

I swallowed hard at hearing my full name for the first time in as long as I could remember.

"Is that you? Tell me where you are."

I hung up the phone as tears fell free from my lashes.

I hurried to the bathroom and grabbed my dirty clothes and a keycard from the small envelope on the stand. I scribbled out a note for Rellik and left it on the desk, even though it would probably be hours until he came back.

I slipped my feet into my sneakers, stepping on the backs as I shuffled down the front of the building to a lit alcove between the rooms. To the right was an ice machine and several snack machines. To the left was a laundry room and small indoor pool.

One older woman in a sweat suit was doing laundry. She smiled as I walked by her and slipped my clothes into the machine.

"Shit," I groaned as I noticed the coin slot.

"You need some help?"

"I forgot my purse. My boyfriend ran to the store and I left it in the car." It was better than the awkward truth that I was staying in a stranger's room.

"Here." She dug through her bag and pulled out several quarters.

"Thank you so much." I stuck them in the slot and glanced over at her machine as I chewed my lip.

"I guess you need soap too?"

I nodded feeling like a complete jerk but she just smiled and held out her small sample size bottle to share.

"Thank you so much. That's incredibly kind of you."

I used what I needed and started the small load as we fell silent, Rellik's singing playing over and over in my head. You could tell he felt every single lyric and I wondered what could have happened to him.

By the time my laundry was washed and dried I was exhausted and ready to curl up in bed.

CHAPTER TWELVE

RELLIK
SELF-PRESERVATION

**Self-Preservation: a natural or instinctive tendency
to act so as to preserve one's own existence.**

I had grown tired of Phantom's glares as some emaciated redhead with fake tits grinded her boney ass against me to the beat of Sail playing in the background. The guys didn't know I had Ella back in my room and I was happy to keep it a secret but I couldn't wait to get the hell out of there and make sure she was okay. I drained what was left in my glass of Jameson and tried to pretend I was interested in the woman in front of me. I closed my eyes and the room began to spin.

"I have to call it a night," I smacked the girl's ass and she jumped from my lap.

"What's the rush?"

I groaned as I stood, rolling my neck from side to side before responding to Phantom. "It's three in the fucking morning and I have to visit family tomorrow."

He nodded and took a drink from his bottle of Budweiser. "I'll catch a ride."

"I'll ride you, baby." The redhead sauntered seductively across the room to Phantom.

I stumble-stepped out of the door and down the long winding hallways until I found the exit into the humid morning air. The oppressive wall of humidity turned my stomach.

I blared 3 Doors Down as I made my way towards the hotel, becoming more alert the closer I got. I parked directly in front of my room.

I slid the key card into the hotel door and opened it slowly. The light was off but the television was still on and turned down low. Ella was in the bed, her dark hair splayed across the white pillow. She was wearing one of my vintage band t-shirts and a pair of boxers and I could smell my cologne in the air.

My eyes danced down her long legs to a small dream catcher tattoo on her ankle.

I stumbled across the room and slipped into the bathroom, my hand pressed against the wall for balance. Taking off my t-shirt I glanced at the mirror over the sink at the slight swelling of my lower lip. I slid my jeans and boxers down over my hips as I kicked off my shoes. Catching myself on the door frame as I began to lose my balance.

I kicked my clothing to the side and took a quick shower to wash the sweat from my body as I thought over the day. I was exhausted and needed to sleep but the hotel had no rooms available because of a convention in town this weekend. I should have told Ella that before but I was afraid she wouldn't stay and I didn't know what would happen to her.

I wrapped a towel around my waist and quietly made my way to my duffle bag and I glanced over to the bed where Ella lay unmoving. I unzipped my duffle bag and pulled out a pair of basketball shorts. I dropped the towel and tugged them on as my eyes continued to drift over her as she laid on her side. She is here and she is safe. I should have gone back to the bar. But as she rolled over, whimpering as her eyes blinked open, I froze, suspended between memories and reality.

"Sorry. I didn't mean to wake you. I came to check on you and my stuff was in here." The lies rolled easier off my tongue than the truth. When you spent as much time as I did concealing your true self, it took no effort.

"No, it's fine." She sat up and pushed her hair from her face as she yawned. "How was the party?"

"Boring." I tried not to stare at her legs as she stretched, rolling my neck from side to side. "So, you wanna talk about what happened earlier… with that guy?"

She shook her head as she tucked her hair behind her ear. "I really don't know where he came from. I went home to change between shifts and he was just there… waiting."

"What are you going to do once we leave? You can't really be sleeping on the streets or hanging out in dark alleys."

"I met you in a dark alley and you're not so bad." She shrugged and I laughed sardonically. I was a curse, a black cloud. It was a slide of hand. I hadn't saved her, but lured her into my own web. She wanted to feel like she could trust me and all of this was on her terms, but I didn't even trust myself.

"Maybe he wasn't the one you needed to watch out for." Subtle truths slipped through, veiled in sarcasm. It was the only warning she would get. I wasn't strong enough to walk away.

"I'll take my chances." She stretched her arms over her head as she yawned, bowing her back forward. I couldn't help but notice her small breasts pressed against the thin fabric of my shirt. I wished I had chosen something that would conceal a hard-on better than these shorts. "I was trying to save up to go back home but now I will have to start all over." She pulled her legs to her chest and wrapped her arms around them, hugging herself.

"Where's home?"

"Technically here but I don't really remember much of it. I left when I was little. My grandmother used to live in Jacksonville before she passed. I've always wanted to go back and buy her place just in case," she sighed as she rested her cheek on her knees.

"Just in case what?" My chest tightened as I thought about the memories I'd left behind and how hard it was to come back. I didn't like how personal things turned with her.

"It's silly," she waved her hand as if to dismiss the conversation but I knew there was something deep lurking below the calm surface and I wanted to know more.

"What happened after your grandma died?"

"That's a few years I'd like to forget. So what about you? Are all of you from here?"

"Just me."

"How did you guys meet?"

I closed my eyes and pinched the bridge of my nose at the onslaught of memories. "It's really late." Liquor was still pumping through my veins and if I didn't end this conversation I would end up saying more than I wanted.

"Oh," Ella pulled her lip between her teeth as she looked up at me quizzically, biting back whatever question was plaguing her.

"What?"

"What's your real name? It's kind of weird I'm sleeping in your bed and don't even know who you really are."

"Many women have slept in my bed without knowing who I really am. You don't want to know and you don't need to know." I cursed myself in my head. I'd just reduced Ella to a notch in a fucking headboard.

"Fair enough." If I'd offended her, she didn't let it show she pushed from the bed and stood in front of me, stretching again. My shirt she wore rode above the waist of the boxers that she had rolled down to sit low on her hips. There was something incredibly sexy seeing her crawl out of my bed in my clothes.

"Are you hungry or need anything?" I tried to keep my eyes on hers, but my gaze travelled down her chest as I grew hard. The air around us began to change and it was suddenly very apparent that we were locked alone in a bedroom. My self-control only went so far. I wasn't that love-sick little boy anymore. My scars ran much deeper than anyone had seen.

"I could use something to drink," she replied.

"Trigger has a few bottles. His room is upstairs. I could grab something. What's your poison?"

Her eyes travelled up my naked torso and locked on to mine before glancing to my mouth as she took a step closer to me, her fingers touching the bracelet Katie had made me. *Poison.* That's exactly what I was to a girl like her, like Katie, the first and last girl that I had kissed. It was a move I couldn't counter. I had to walk away. I didn't want to use Ella like all of the other women in my life.

"I should go," my voice trailed off as I rubbed my palm across my jaw and turned away from her so I wouldn't be tempted to act on my impulses. "Before he falls asleep." My tone was harsher than I intended but Phantom's concerns replayed in my head. He wasn't worried for me. He was worried about Ella and I should be too. As strong as she pretended she was, she had no sense of self-preservation. Her pride clouded her judgment, much like in the alleyway. She would have died fighting that prick before she screamed for help. I dug through my bag for a t-shirt as I talked myself into walking away.

"I don't want alcohol." Ella put her hand on my shoulder and I turned around to face her, her eyebrows drawn together in rejection. I wanted so desperately to kiss away the worries that marred her perfect face. I wanted to slip into the fantasy of the past haunting me, but I knew it was something I'd never recover from.

"I know what you want. I can't give it to you." I walked around her and out the door before she could respond. The night air was muggy as I sank down into a crouching position with my hands together. She wasn't Katie. I needed to get that through my head so it is easier to walk away when we leave town. What happened to her after that wasn't my problem. I wasn't going to be able to protect her and she didn't want me to. Worrying myself over that wasn't doing me any favors. Fucking her would be a big mistake, even if it was all I wanted to do.

The door opened behind me and Ella slipped out. Dressed in her own clothing, her arms were around herself as she stepped off the curb and began walking across the parking lot. She was leaving, like I'd hoped and it set my mind into a panic.

"Where are you going," I called after her but she kept walking. "Ella?" I stood as she made her way through the rows of cars, desperately trying to talk myself out of following her. "Fuck." I walked after her, the gravel biting into the soles of my feet.

I had to jog to catch up with her before she reached the road. Grabbing her arm, I stopped her and turned her to face me. Her voice was strained as she began to ramble, "I made a mistake coming here. I'm sorry I screwed up your night. I appreciate your help, but I'm not your problem. Just let me go before I humiliate myself any further." She tugged against my grip but I tightened it so she wouldn't leave.

"I'm sorry if I hurt your feelings. That wasn't my intention." My eyes searched hers before I took a deep breath, sinking deeper into the lies that now clouded my reality. "I've been through a lot. I've… done a lot of things that I'm not proud of."

"We all have regrets."

"I don't regret *anything*." I shook my head, the muscles in my jaw flexing as I clenched my teeth. "I'm not your fucking hero, Ella. I'm no better than that asshole who attacked you." I snapped, hating the animal I had become. Doing the right thing wasn't something I was accustomed to. I was trying desperately not to slip back into the past, but I only had so much strength. I was far weaker than I let on.

"Maybe I don't want you to be my hero." Her words were challenging and her eyes narrowed as she brushed her long hair from her face angrily, my dick responding to the subtle gesture. I'd wanted to run my fingers through her hair all night. I fought the urge to slam her up against one of these cars and show her exactly what she was asking from me. "Did you ever think of that? Maybe I just wanted to forget everything for five God damn minutes. But you've reminded me of *exactly* who I am."

I was using what happened earlier as an excuse when the real problem was me. It wasn't fair and damn sure wasn't what I wanted. I closed the small gap between us, my bare chest pressed against hers. I towered over her but she straightened her back and stood tall. My free hand ghosted over her cheek, sliding it into her soft hair before gripping it tightly and tugging her head back, forcing her to look up at me. "Five minutes? I'm insulted."

Her lips curved slightly with amusement. She was playing a dangerous game. She thought she wanted control but didn't really understand what it entailed. Her power over the situation was an illusion that I let her believe. I was good at reading people. Most didn't put in the effort she had to mask her true intentions, but I could see it all in her eyes. She wanted me to make her feel special. The chase was what turned her on, made her feel safe. She had no idea how special she really was.

"Prove me wrong." She raised her eyebrow, challenging me. She was playing cat and mouse with a motherfucking lion.

I was about to cross a line and there was nothing harmless about me. I wasn't a tortured artist with the need to express my feelings though music. I was the fucking devil incarnate, biding my time and waiting for the chance to avenge my loss. Our eyes searched each other's, the green ripping my heart out with every beat, as I slowly lowered my mouth to hers. Her lips were soft and I pressed harder against her as I inhaled the sweet memory of cherry ChapStick. Her head tilted as lips parted to allow me access. My hand fell from her arm to her lower back as I pulled her body tight against mine, my tongue sweeping over her lower lip as I drank her in. Her own tongue pressed back against mine, deepening our kiss. She wasn't timid and her urgency pulled me into the moment and out of my thoughts. I kept my fingers tangled in her hair as my other hand moved lower, sliding over her ass. Her own hands were on my sides, holding me against her, the evidence of how much I wanted her pressed against her stomach. She wasn't wearing a bra and her nipples hardened against me.

"You want me to stop treating you like you're breakable? It stops now." I lifted her, her legs wrapping around me as I turned, sitting her down on the hood of a car, her skirt pushed up over her hips. I slid my hand under her tank top, palming her breast in my hand as I continued to kiss her. I was desperate to feel her, outside and in. I'd never wanted to fuck someone so badly and I was willing to do it in the middle of a parking lot.

She whimpered as I rocked my hips against her, her panties and my shorts doing little to keep us apart. Her hands were on my back and she pulled me towards her from her own desperation.

"Come back to the room so I can take my time fucking you," I mumbled against her lips, my body humming with anticipation. Fuck trying to be the good guy. If I couldn't save myself, no one else would be safe. She nodded and reluctantly broke away from our kiss, her thumb wiping over her lower lip. *Fuck* she was sexy and nothing like the others, too bad she was like the one I needed to forget.

I straightened and held my hand out for hers. She took it and I pulled her to her feet. She giggled as she pulled her skirt down over her hips, as she realized what we had just done in public.

Ella walked by me and back toward the room, her hips rocking with each step. I followed after her, as she slipped her hand into her messenger bag and pulled out the key card to the room.

"You knew I'd come after you." I narrowed my eyes as she slipped it into the card slot and pushed the door open without speaking a word.

"I hoped."

"Be careful what you wish for." I waited for her to enter before following her into the cool air. I stood just inside of the door as she faced me, dropping her purse and sliding the bag off her shoulders to the floor as she kicked off her sandals. Her hands moved quickly, undoing her jean skirt as she slid it over her hips but her fingers gave away her nervousness. It was such a fucking turn on to see her act so brave when I knew this wasn't something she would normally do. I was glad. The idea of her doing this with other men would have killed the moment for me, even though there was no reason for me to give a fuck who or what she did.

"Are you on something?" I asked, not wanting any physical barrier between us. She nodded and I took two large strides towards her. My arms slipped around her back, gripping her ass as I pulled her against me and onto her toes. My mouth was on hers, hungry to be closer, desperate to be inside of her and lost in a memory.

I grabbed her tank top and pulled it roughly over her sending her hair cascading over small breasts. She looked to the ground for a moment, unsure of herself. If she had any doubt of how fucking incredible she looked, the evidence was stiff and obvious under my shorts. I gripped my cock through the fabric, desperate for some relief. She pushed against my shoulders and I walked backwards until I was against the wall. Her lips pressed against my chest. I wanted nothing more than to let her continue her journey lower, but if I was going to hell, I'd make the trip worth it.

I grabbed her shoulders and turned, pressing her back against the wall with a little more force than necessary. A wicked grin spread across her face as I bent down to taste her mouth again, my fingers digging hard into the flesh of her upper thighs.

CHAPTER THIRTEEN

ELLA
POSSESSIVE

Possessive: demanding someone's total attention and love.

His fingertips gripped me possessively. I loved the burn, the idea of his marks lingering on my flesh long after this night was over, a reminder of being wanted by someone who was wanted by all. My own fingers slid over his chest and I dug my nails into his flesh causing him to growl, his teeth biting down on my lower lip.

"Fuck," he whispered as his right hand left my hip and rested tenderly against my cheek, but he pressed harder against me and I could feel every inch of what I was doing to him and my clit throbbed at the contact. "Look at me."

My hands slid further up, circling behind his neck and into his hair, my nails scratching a path into his skin and he growled against my lips. I reluctantly met his gaze, hating the intimacy of it. At such a vulnerable moment I felt like all of my secrets were being exposed.

Both his hands were under my thighs and he lifted me from my feet, my back hitting the wall again and his length torturing me as he pressed against my center. I wrapped my legs around his body, holding him close as he slid against me slowly, and his eyes never leaving mine.

He was rough and careless like the man I'd met in the shadows of that alley, the one with mercy in his eyes but murder in his intent.

His muscles flexed and stretched, his hands brutalizing flashed through my mind as his lips left mine, sucking and biting the sensitive flesh below my ear. He was raw and aggressive. I could hear myself panting, my eyes closed as I pushed back against him, desperate for release, but not wanting to rush this moment. He wanted this as badly as I did, but he was taking his time.

His tongue ran from the base of my neck to my ear lobe, his breathing as ragged as mine, ragged as it had been when he helped me.

"You are nothing like I'd imagined," he growled in my ear, his hips rolling forward causing a whimper to escape my lips.

"You imagined fucking me?" My voice was low and raw with passion. He gripped on to me tightly and carried me to the bed, my legs still wrapped around him. We tumbled down together, his body causing the air to expel from my lungs, but I was breathless long before we collided.

"It's all I've done since the moment I met you."

There was an urgency now, a need growing deep inside of me, spreading like warm whiskey through my veins. I was intoxicated by his touch. Fingers slid under my white cotton panties, as he gripped them tightly and tugged. My own hands ran over his back, relishing in every twist and pull of his muscles as he moved against me. Those same muscles he used to defend me just hours before were now desperate to conquer me. The same animalistic current running through them that now ran through me.

My panties gave way to his force, ripping free. The scrap of fabric now laying loosely over me, dampened and torn. My own hands travelled lower, running along the waist of his shorts. The silky fabric doing little to contain him. He pushed the torn remnants of my underwear to the side, groaning as his fingers slid over my smooth, damp flesh.

"You're wet for me." His mouth moved lower, kissing the center of my chest before running his tongue over my nipple and pulling it into his mouth. My back arched toward him, fingers in his hair as he bit down on the milky colored flesh of my breast. I gasped and just as quickly he released his teeth and ran his tongue over the fresh pink crescent mark. His eyes met mine, challenging me. I didn't fight against him. The control was his to have as long as he didn't stop.

His fingertips ran lightly over the small, thin scars that marred my lower belly and thighs. "Who hurt you?"

"Who hurt *you*?" I asked as he gaze lingered on me for a few seconds and he pressed his lips gently against one of the marks.

"That's a long list." Pressing open mouth kisses on my tingling skin, he made his way lower. I raised my hips, desperate for him to settle between my thighs. I felt his lips curve into a smile as he grabbed my hips tightly and pulled them back against the mattress.

"You're so mean," I panted as I struggled against his hold.

"You have no idea." He dipped lower his teeth grazing my inner thigh before he bit again, this time a little harder. I whimpered, struggling to raise my hips again but he held me firmly in place as he kissed the mark he had left behind and his unshaved cheek brushed against my mound sending a shiver through my body.

"God," I turned my head to the side, my eyes closed tightly.

"Ella," his voice was rough and low like when he sings and I could have melted into a puddle from that alone. I looked down at him, his blue eyes searched my face before he slowly lowered his mouth to me. His eyes never left mine as he pressed his tongue against my slit and slowly dragged it upward and over my clit. The stubble of his jaw against my bare flesh was overwhelming. "You taste *so* fucking good."

His hand left my hip and he spread me open with his fingers and his mouth was back against me, forcefully. He growled as he devoured me with his mouth and the vibrations nearly cause me to come undone. My hands were back in his hair, my back arched as I moved against his tongue. Suddenly he entered me with his fingers, groaning as he slid them rhythmically inside of me. "You're fucking tight, Ella." He shook his head before pressing his tongue against me again. I relaxed a little, my body moving against him on its own accord.

"I want you to watch me do this to you." As our eyes met his tongue ran painfully slow over my clit and I whimpered. My eyes falling closed again, wanting to be lost in the moment. "You can't beg me to fuck you and then pretend to be shy."

I pushed up on my elbows, embarrassed. "I didn't *beg* you."

He grinned mischievously as he crawled up my body, forcing me back against the mattress. "Maybe I should make you. I'd love to see you on your knees." He pulled down the front of his basketball shorts, gripping himself in his palm. "I don't think you knew what you were asking for." His length was impressive and I didn't know if I'd even be able to take all of him in my mouth, if that's what he wanted. He hovered over me, on his elbow as he pressed his cock against my clit. "Imagine how good it is going to feel when I slide inside of you." He lowered his weight fractionally as he pressed harder against me, his stomach muscles tight and offering me the sexiest view I'd ever seen between us.

CHAPTER FOURTEEN

RELLIK
SELF-CONTROL

Self-Control: The ability to control oneself, in particular one's emotions and desires or the expression of them in one's behavior, especially in difficult situations.

I wanted to fuck her so badly but I was enjoying this too much. It wasn't often a women challenged me and I loved pushing her past her comfort zone.

I could understand her apprehension to look me in the eye. I couldn't even tell you what most of the girls I had slept with looked like, but Ella's emerald gaze was like a fucking dagger in my heart and I liked the hurt. I wanted to feel it because at least with the pain I knew I was alive, knew I was still able to feel *something*.

I slid the head of my cock lower and positioned myself against her entrance. "I can't promise I won't hurt you." I felt her thigh muscles tighten against me slightly and I knew that as badly as I wanted to ravage her, I would need to keep some semblance of control over myself. She wasn't like the groupies and her slight frame would not help our situation.

I rocked against her slowly as I lowered my body against hers. My head slipping inside of her. "You have to relax." I lowered my mouth to hers, growing even harder as she tasted her own juices on my tongue. I pressed forward, desperate to come, but her body tensed and I knew it was too much. "Relax, Ella. Relax."

"I'm trying. It's not like I do this all the time."

"That makes two of us."

She laughed and I raised myself up to look at her face. "I'm fucking serious."

"You don't have to lie to make me feel better. It's none of my business."

I pulled completely out of her, wincing as I did so, my dick still hard as rock. I pulled my shorts over me, the silky fabric against my head enough to make me cringe. Climbing off her, I sat on the edge of the bed.

"Ella, I do a lot of things I shouldn't, but when I have my cock inside of you, I'm not going to lie just to get fucked." I was trying to bite back my anger. Her words wouldn't have even affected me had she been someone else, but the truth was, I rarely had actual sex with any of the groupies and I sure as fuck didn't waste my time going down on them.

"I'm sorry." She grabbed the blanket and pulled it over herself as she sat up behind me.

I rested my elbows on my knees as I ran my hand over my hair, wishing my cock would take a back seat to my actual feelings. "Don't be. We shouldn't have been doing this. You'd be sorry tomorrow had I not stopped."

I pushed from the bed and began pacing the floor. I watched her out of the corner of my eye as she crawled further toward the headboard and laid on her back, the cover down to her waist.

"I guess I'll just have to take care of myself."

I shook my head in disbelief as she slid her hand under the cover, her lips parting slightly as she kept her eyes locked on mine. "Are you trying to fucking kill me?" I asked, my hand sliding in my shorts as I gripped myself tightly. Her nipples pebbled and she slid her free hand over one of her breasts, squeezing it as her back arched.

"You are so sexy," I whispered as I began to stroke myself, my thumb sliding over my head, still wet from her juices. My words gave her confidence and the cover slipped a little lower, still hiding her pussy from my view.

"Come back to bed," she whimpered as her hand moved faster. I began to stroke at her pace but didn't move closer.

"I'd fucking hurt you, Ella. I can't control myself right now."

She groaned and it took all of my self-control not to hold her down and slam myself inside of her. "I'd let you."

"Fuck," I slid my hand down over my balls as they drew closer to my body, desperate for release. I pushed my shorts lower so she could see what she was doing to me. I wasn't shy by any means. "I want to see how you're touching yourself while thinking of me."

Kicking the cover lower I watched as her fingertips pressed against her clit, her back arching with every rub. I pushed my shorts to the floor and walked to the end of the bed. She began to pull her legs together and I grabbed her ankle, shaking my head as I began to stroke faster. "I want to watch you come."

"Please," she whimpered.

"What do you need, sweetheart?"

"Please come back to bed and fuck me."

"If you're going to beg," I couldn't help the little dig as I climbed between her legs, pausing to run my tongue over her wet fingers as they slid over herself before settling over her. My dick pressed against her hand as my mouth found hers, kissing her hard.

Damp fingers wrapped around the head of my cock, guiding me lower as I pressed against her entrance. I rocked my hips slowly but our kiss was anything but cautious and it was a struggle to keep myself under control.

Nails dug into the flesh of my back as she pulled me against her and I entered her, painfully slow.

She whimpered against my lips but didn't loosen her hold on me. I slid my fingers into her hair, unable to breath. I was killing myself but I couldn't stop. It was a slow motion car crash that I had no way of surviving. I would take her down with me and she would willingly go. Something broken inside of both of us fit together, the jagged pieces piercing into the armor we wore against the world.

"Are you okay?" Whispering into her hair I slowed my movements slightly.

"I'm not going to break."

"Am I hurting you?'

"It's a good hurt."

She was a flame, I was gasoline and together we burned, an inferno so hot it would consume us both.

Our bodies moved together, demanding and greedy, as we both struggled to fill some void inside of us. This line should have never been crossed but over the hours it had become blurred, past and present infused as one. Her breathing grew ragged as my fingers tightened in her hair, the faint sound of counting whispered in my ear. I stopped, pulling back to look at her.

"Why are you counting?" I rubbed the pad of my thumb over her eyebrow and her expression relaxed.

"I didn't realize I was. It's just something I do some- times when I'm…" her eyes searched as if she was looking for the answer written on the wall.

"Scared?"

"Overwhelmed," she swallowed hard and I nodded fractionally, understanding exactly where she was com- ing from. Our bodies began to move again, slower as the gravity of the situation seemed to literally hold us down. I didn't know what it was she had been through, but I could tell it rivaled my own experiences.

Her legs wrapped around my waist, allowing me to go deeper, her lips against my ear as her breathing hitched, her body tightening around me. I kept pace as she began to whimper in my ear, her body shaking as she came completely undone and I followed.

CHAPTER FIFTEEN

ELLA
CHAOTIC

Chaotic: In a state of complete confusion and disorder.

I laid beside Rellik, wide awake, my mind unable to shut down after such a chaotic day. I rolled to my side, away from him and my eyes landed on the black duffle bag on top of the corner desk.

I held my breath as I listened to his slow and steady breathing. My curiosity getting the best of me, I slowly sat up and pressed a foot to the floor. I froze, waiting for any movement from his side, but he was out cold. I placed my other foot on the floor and slowly stood, my eyes dancing over the bag. I wanted read more of his lyrics, to see what made him the way he was.

Grabbing the zipper, I slowly began to pull it open, but the sound was deafening in the quiet space and Rellik stirred, rolling away from me. I sighed, closing my eyes and whispering a silent prayer before slowly closing it back up. I ran my hand through my knotted hair before laughing and making my way into the bathroom. I turned on the light, momentarily blinded by the fluorescents.

When I was able to focus on the mirror I cringed at just how horrible I looked. I combed my fingers through my hair, desperate to make myself look a little less of a mess. As I took a step back to examine myself I stepped on something and nearly lost my balance.

Glancing down I realized that I had trampled Rellik's dirty clothing. I picked up his jeans and slid my hand into the bulging back pocket, pulling out a brown snakeskin wallet. I glanced toward the open bathroom door before flipping it open. There were quite a few bills in the money slot as well as a business card for Silver Lake Psychiatric Facility. It was well worn like it had been in his wallet for years. Why the hell would he have a card like this? The smaller pockets held movie stubs, a hotel key card, and a picture of a girl who looked startlingly like me. I glanced up at my face in the mirror and back at the picture.

I slid the picture back in and pulled out his driver's license. My eyes danced over the information typed beside his picture. "Ryder Bentley," I whispered under my breath as I my heart felt like it was going to explode from my chest. How was it possible? Of all the people to run into? It was chance. It had to be. The warnings from Phantom began to make sense. I dropped the wallet onto the ground and it made a loud clapping sound as it hit the tile. My hand was over my mouth now and I struggled to keep my composure. Who the hell did I just sleep with?

Falling against the door frame, my eyes struggled to adjust to the darkness of the room. I pulled clothing from my bag and struggled to get dressed in a pair of jeans and fitted t-shirt before Rellik woke.

I didn't have a plan but I knew it was now or never if I wanted answers.

CHAPTER SIXTEEN

RELLIK
CRAZY

Crazy – A mentally deranged person.

"Where is she?"

I wiped the sleep from my eyes as I sat up, groaning from exhaustion. The voice grew louder from down the hall. I made my way to the front door to see who the woman was yelling. She looked exhausted, still wearing pajamas. Her eyes locked onto mine. "Tell me where Katie is right now!"

"She's not here, Janet."

"I know about you liking my daughter! Bryce told me all about it," she spat angrily, my mother stepping in front of her. "Tell me where she is or I'm calling the police!"

"He told you he doesn't know," Mr. Thomas stepped in front of me, folding his arms over his chest. I was thankful someone was finally taking my side.

"How long has she been missing?" I stepped around Mr. Thomas, my concern for Katie growing.

"Like you don't know."

"I don't. I haven't been able to talk to her since…" I shook my head as I placed my hand on my mother's shoulder. "My phone. Where is it?"

My mother's looked down the hallway behind me before pushing by and heading for the kitchen. She returned a moment later with my phone in hand. As it turned on it began to beep as messages came through. I snatched the phone from her hands, my eyes dancing over the rapid fire texts. Katie was desperate to see me and I knew exactly where she had went to meet me. I shoved by her mother practically knocking her down the front steps as I took off into the dark just as the rain began to fall.

I reached the woods, breathless and terrified. Pulling my phone from my pocket, I dialed her number as I made my way through the trees. Approaching our spot, I could hear the faint ringing of her phone but she wasn't answering. I yelled her name, shoving the phone into my pocket as I made my way into the small clearing, stopping short of Katie, lying on the ground, partially submerged in a puddle of blood and rain.

"Get up! Get up now," A frantic voice called from what sounded like a tunnel. I blinked open blurry, eyes and focused on the beautiful brunette in front of me, her eyes pleading with me but I wasn't sure what it was she wanted. "Get up! Get the hell up!"

"Katie," I groaned, each word melting into the next like liquid as I struggled to stop the room from spinning, thankful I wasn't in the woods on the day my world came crashing down.

She grabbed my arm with her hand, her nails digging into the flesh of my bicep.

"Ouch! Fuck!" I sat up and ran my hand over my eyes. "Ella? What the fuck happened? Are you alright?" Her other hand shook as she gripped onto a small silver gun. "Whoa! Where did you get that?"

"I told you I had a gun in my purse," Her voice was shaky as she spoke but her finger was on the trigger. She was looking at me now, the real me. I could feel it like a coldness that crept down to my bones.

"So you did," I sat up slowly, my open palm toward her so she knew I wasn't going to hurt her. "Why is it pointed at *me*?"

"You tell me, *Ryder.*"

"You went through my things?" I took a deep breath and tried to swallow back my anger. "Why did you do that? Were you stealing from me?"

"Oh, you don't get to feel violated." Both hands gripped the gun to steady it.

"So you know my name." My eyes darted to my duffle bag. "What else do you know?"

Her eyes followed mine.

"What's with the card for the Psych Ward? You're fucking crazy?"

"You're holding me at gunpoint and are questioning my sanity?" She wasn't asking the real question.

"Do I sound like I'm joking with you? Who's the girl?"

"What girl?" I shook my head, slowly leaning a little more forward. There it was, the question that was burning in her mind.

"The girl in the picture who looks just like me. Why do you have it?"

I ran my hand over my mouth, biting back the curse I wanted to unleash. "Question time is over. Either pull the fucking trigger, come back to bed or leave."

"No! I have the gun so I am in charge."

This wasn't going to end well, but I knew that before I slept with her.

My eyes narrowed as I slowly reached forward so I wouldn't startle her. I wrapped my hands around hers as she gripped the gun and pulled her toward me until the cold barrel pressed against my bare chest. "Do it," I whispered. "Fucking do it. Tell the world some crazy asshole locked you in his hotel room and forced himself on you. Trust me, they'll believe you. But that's not what happened, Ella. The truth is, you came back to my hotel room *willingly*. You spread your legs for a fucking stranger without even knowing his God damn name. You practically fucking *begged* me for it. And now you're the one holding a gun and calling *me* crazy?" Her grip loosened and I slid the weapon from her hand. I immediately grabbed her shoulders and flipped over so I was on top of her, pinning her arms next to her head. I adjusted her arms so I was able to grip her wrists in one hand above her head, my other hand against her neck, forcing her to look me in the eye.

"You want to kill me, Ella? Huh? You want to fucking *kill* me?" My grip tightened as she struggled to turn her head, my finger tips on her jaw so as to not cut off her air supply. Our lips were practically touching and under different circumstances her heavy panting would have turned me on.

"I didn't pull the trigger."

"You fucking should have because if you *ever* pull a stunt like that again," My voice trailed off as her eyes filled with tears. "Don't. You don't get to be sad. You don't get to be a fucking victim. YOU PUT A FUCKING GUN TO MY HEART!"

"I'm *not* a victim," her eyes narrowed, tears running down into her hair.

I bit back my rage and lowered my voice so my words wouldn't fall on deaf ears. "That girl… that girl in the picture…" I squeezed my eyes closed momentarily trying to calm my racing thoughts. I never talked about Katie to anyone. Her memories were mine alone. "*She* was a victim. She was… *everything* to me and she is dead because of it."

I felt the column of her throat move under my palm as she swallowed hard, her heart racing under my fingers.

"So if you want to play the victim with me, Ella, I will fucking make you one." I kept her gaze for a moment before slowly releasing my grip on her hands. Her fingers immediately went to the hand that circled her throat, gripping tightly over the bracelet Katie had made me.

Chapter Seventeen

ELLA
ERRATIC

Erratic: Unpredictable.

I struggled to calm my breathing, counting erratically as Rellik pushed from the bed and grabbed his shorts, yanking them on as he cursed under his breath. He paced the floor for a moment before he wondered into the bathroom, slamming his hands against the tile, biting out a curse that sounded like a roar. I didn't have a second to waste as I pushed from the bed and ran for the door. I flung it open, letting it bounce hard off the wall behind it, the sound echoing through the room as I took off in a full sprint, barefoot and without any of my things. As I hit the rows of cars, I struggled against the urge to continue on, instead I ducked down between the vehicles, pressing my back against the wheel of an old maroon Cadillac.

"Ella," he called out in an eerily playful tone. I put my hands over my mouth to calm my breathing as I closed my eyes, my mind immediately taking me back to those days I had hid inside my closet and begged to not be found. "You're really beginning to piss me the fuck off."

His voice grew closer as I crawled behind the vehicle and stilled at the rear end of a jeep.

"You surprise me. But I bet I could surprise you too." I could hear his muffled footsteps nearby. "When I heard from Maric that someone was digging into my past, initially I was pissed. That chapter of my life was closed. But when I saw your face, I couldn't believe it. It fucked up my head, Ella. I almost didn't come back to find out why you were so interested in me. But I never really had a choice. You knew that already didn't you?"

I kept my body pressed against the bumper of the jeep, the sun slowly rising and illuminating the world around me. If I ran he'd catch me. I had no choice but to wait it out and hope for some divine intervention.

"What are the odds of me being there to save you in that alley? I mean, you'd probably have a better chance of hitting the lottery. I know what you're thinking, I was there buying some pills and it was just an odd coincidence. I gave myself a plausible reason to be there. I also showed you that my reasoning was validated. It's actually quite easy to push someone into trusting you when you don't have a lot of time." He laughed and my stomach turned. How could I not know who he really was? "I never expected that asshole to put his hands on you. That wasn't part of the plan. I guess it was a good thing I was there... watching you." His voice was somber and he grew quiet for a moment. "The eviction was simple. Did you know you can buy those signs almost anywhere? You should really learn about tenants' rights, Ella, because that isn't how the process works. But at eighteen who can really blame you for being so *fucking* stupid."

He began to walk again and I struggled to crawl, stones digging into my knees and palms as I rounded another vehicle.

"Your landlord may be pissed about those screw holes in your door, but since you haven't paid your rent in a while, I'm sure I only expedited the process."

I began counting under my breath, struggling to keep my words silent as I begged my heart rate to slow.

"You want me to keep going? It's really quite impressive. I've got to tell you, I was a little fucking pissed about Phantom sticking his nose in my God damn business. He never really did understand what it was like to love someone. It doesn't go away, even after death."

I pushed to my feet, still hunched over as I darted to the next row of cars. His steps grew closer and I squeezed my eyes closed, begging I wouldn't be found.

"To be honest, all of those years spent in Silver Lake had an impact, albeit minimal. I made some friends… you know the guys. I focused on my music, I fucked every dumb fucking cunt who spread her legs."

His hands wrapped around my wrists and pulled me to my feet as I yelp in shock, my eyes flying open and staring into his. The vibrant blue of calm waters now dark like a raging storm. They were vacant now. The compassion he'd shown earlier drowned in the murkiness of his past.

"Then there was you," He whispered in a hushed tone as his eyes searched mine. "It was… fate."

"It wasn't fate. You lied to me." I shook my head, hoping that I would somehow wake myself from the nightmare I had walked right into.

"You sought *me* out. You wanted to find *me*, Ella. Why? If you knew about my past why where you looking for me?"

"So you don't have it all figured out?"

"Ella Leighton has no past, no identity past a few months ago. You get paid under the table, you paid rent in cash, when you paid it at all. The utilities were all in the landlord's name. It's like you're a ghost. Like you're *her* ghost."

"I needed to find out the truth."

"The truth about what?" His grip tightened when I didn't respond. "About what?" his voice rose with anger.

"Hey? What's going on over there?" A stranger's voice broke through our conversation and he reluctantly let go of me, tears in my eyes, answers on the tip of my tongue.

"Ella," his eyes searched mine but I shook my head fractionally before I took off, weaving between cars and across the main road. He wouldn't be stupid enough to chase after me in broad daylight with witnesses. I had no idea where I was even going. My apartment was no longer safe and I wasn't any closer to finding out the truth, but part of me knew that regardless of intent, Rellik was at least partially responsible for the torture I'd suffered for years.

CHAPTER EIGHTEEN

RELLIK
CONNECTION

Connection: A relationship in which a person, thing or idea is linked or associated with something else.

I couldn't see straight, the ache of having to stand there and watch her walk away was more than I had anticipated. I clenched my jaw as I reluctantly made my way across the now lit parking lot to my room. Banging my fist off the door I bit out a curse when I realized I didn't have my key card and would have to go to the office.

I walked along the narrow sidewalk to the main entrance and pulled open the door, the air conditioning reminding me that I had left in such a hurry I forgot to put on a shirt.

The women behind the desk blushed as my eyes met hers and she immediately looked down to her computer, a smirk on her face.

"Can I help you with something, Sir?"

"I locked myself out of my room. I need a key card."

"Certainly. What is your room number?"

"119."

"You're checking out today? Would you like a copy of your bill?"

"Nah. I didn't order any room service. Should be pretty straight forward." I was leaving early today to get a room closer to my mom's house. I didn't want to assume they'd want me to stay with open arms and I wasn't sure I could handle the memories. It had been years since I've seen her.

"You're right. Only made one phone call." She held out a plastic keycard and I took it, as I thought over what she'd said.

"Actually, I think I'll take the bill. Tax purposes."

"Sure. No problem." With a smile she clicked print and the papers began to shoot out of the printer next to her. I tried to hide my excitement as I took them from her hand. Maybe Ella wasn't as good at covering her trail as she'd thought.

I left the office, the sun blinding and already unbearably hot, to make my way back to my room. The guys wouldn't be up for a few hours, sleeping away their hangovers. I wasn't as lucky. I'd had two hours of sleep if I was lucky and I didn't see any more in my future for a long time.

I had to find the connection between Ella and my past. The fact that she bared such a striking resemblance to Katie only fucked up my head more. That couldn't be explained away and must have had a direct correlation to how she fit in to the story.

I slipped inside my room, scanning Ella's possessions that still laid where she'd left them, like she had stepped out for some fresh air, not ran off in fear of me discovering the truth. My eyes fell to the paper in my hand and I studied the local number. Who would she have called? She claimed to have nowhere else to go, no other place to stay. Was that just to get closer to me? Couldn't have been. The look in her eyes when she discovered my name was genuine. She hadn't known who I really was. You couldn't fake that kind of betrayal. But why the fear? If she'd been tracking me, she should have known exactly what I'd been accused of in the past. Ella had shown little self-preservation in the short time I'd known her. She had too much pride, so it all could be explained away, but it didn't sit right with me. At least now I had a few leads.

I grabbed my cell phone and dialed the number, careful to block my own number. After three rings a man answered, a voice I didn't recognize.

"Hello?" There was some commotion as if adjusting his own phone, and he lowered his voice. "Mikaella? Is that you?"

I disconnected the call and tossed my phone on the bed. Mikaella. At least I'd found another piece to the puzzle. She wasn't very clever with her alias. Who was the man? I turned to the floor and grabbed her book bag, sitting on the bed as I unzipped it, the anticipation causing my heart to race. I pulled out a few outfits, tossing them to the side as I felt around in the bottom of the bag. "Fuck," I growled as my search came up empty. I shoved the clothing back inside and grabbed her purse, dumping the contents onto the covers. I grabbed a card to Lockhart library issued only a few months ago. My heart seized at a newspaper article with Katie's face and I tossed the card on to the covers on top of a picture of Ella as a child. I picked up the article, my eyes struggling to focus on the faded print.

Foul Play Suspected in the Death
of Katie May Alexander

I dropped the paper, letting it flutter to the bed before picking up the next. This was a different case entirely.

Manhunt Expands for the Dream Killer

What did one have to do with the other? Did she think this Dream Killer was responsible for Katie's death? Did she think it was me? Was she some sort of law enforcement that I'd threatened? "Fuck," yelling at the top of my lungs until I had no breath left in my lungs.

"Call the police!" I watched the large silhouette holding her lifeless body walk away, blocking out the light momentarily. What I thought was Heaven was the headlight of a rusted blue pickup truck, God nothing more than a stranger. My angel had forsaken me. I closed my eyes as I quit struggling against the weight on my shoulders. There was no reason for me to fight anymore.

"What did you do to that girl, boy?"

"I loved her." In that moment I realized that it was me who had done this to her. I should have left her alone. I wasn't what she needed and everyone knew it but the two of us. I thought her heart was big enough for the both of us but what we had is what stopped it from beating.

It didn't take long for police cars to swarm the street and in such a small town everyone came out to see what horrific event had transpired. The blue and red lights from the cars bounced off the trees, disorienting me. Handcuffs were placed on my wrists and I was lifted from the ground. As I turned to face everyone I'd ever known, they gasped and screamed as my own eyes drifted down over my blood soaked clothing.

*Hands were all over my body now, searching and grab-
bing at me. "We have a weapon." I turned my head to see
the blood smeared handle of my father's pocket knife. It was
all I had left after losing him and now it had ended the life
of the girl I loved. My eyes turned back to the crowd in time
to see my mother fall to her knees, screaming in agony.*

*"You have the right to remain silent. Anything you say
or do may be used against you in a court of law. You have
the right to consult an attorney before speaking to the police
and to have an attorney present during questioning now or
in the future. If you cannot afford an attorney, one will be
appointed for you before any questioning, if you wish. If
you decide to answer any questions now, without an attorney present, you will still have the right to stop answering
at any time until you talk to an attorney. Do you understand each of these rights I have explained to you?"*

"Yes," I mumbled.

*"Having these rights in mind, do you wish to talk to
us now?"*

*I glanced up at the sound of a woman screaming, my
eyes landing on Katie's mother as Coach held her around
the waist. On her right, was Bryce, no emotion on his face.
I lurched forward as the officer grabbed my arms, struggling to get me on the ground. Another officer helped him,
soon my chest slammed against asphalt, the air momentarily knocked from my lungs.*

*"It's all my fault," I rasped as I rested my cheek against
the warm road.*

Katie's death was ultimately ruled a suicide due to
the vertical cuts on her wrists, but I knew something else
had happened to her, even if the evidence of such a crime

had been washed away. Although as I was proclaimed innocent, I was guilty in the eyes of everyone around me. I couldn't function, couldn't think clearly and was soon sent away to a mental health facility. My mother had suffered enough after the death of my father and I couldn't blame her for not wanting to be the mother of someone everyone thought was a killer. Even if it meant the last person I had in my corner had given up on me.

I crumbled the paper in my hand, cracking my neck as the memories swarmed me, making it impossible to keep myself under control.

A knock at the door got my attention. I shoved the belongings back in the purse and picked up the gun from the bed, tucking it in the back of my shorts. I pressed myself against the door, looking through the peephole, paranoia taking over.

"Housekeeping," An older woman called form the other side.

"No thanks. I'm checking out today," I called back and watched as she shook her head and moved on to the next room.

I grabbed my phone from the bed and did a reverse search on the phone number that Ella had called.

It was a home phone but the owner's name and address wasn't available. I forwarded the number to Trigger.

I need to know who owns this number and where to find them. Keep it on the DL.

A few minutes later he texted me back.

So fucking hung over. I'm on it.

I made my way to my bag, pulling out a clean pair of jeans and my dark blue Lynyrd Skynyrd shirt. Dressing quickly I thought over what had transpired. I couldn't figure out Ella's angle. She looked too young to be with the law. I looked over the gun, it wasn't police issued. I emptied the clip, removing the bullet in the chamber as I thought about it being pointed at my heart. I stuck her gun in her purse and gathered my bag along with the other miscellaneous items around the room before leaving the hotel.

I needed to get across town to my mom's but I walking away from my past had never been easy for me and knowing what I do now about Ella, she was somehow a part of it. In the daylight, the alley where she accessed her apartment looked rundown and desolate.

I parked by the front door and climbed the stairs to her place. The eviction notice was still in place and the lock hadn't been removed. She still may return once she feels the coast is clear. I resisted the urge to find out, instead I hurried down the three flights of stairs and got in my car, pulling off and heading down to Lockhart Library, about five minutes away. Ella would be able to walk here and it was the only other place that I knew she may go. Just the thought of going back home made my stomach turn. I'd been avoiding the prying eyes, the looks of disappointment, and knowing if I ever saw Bryce, I'd finally finish what I'd started.

I'd be lying if I said I didn't think about killing him in just about every way imaginable. He tainted Katie, soiled her innocents and destroyed her life.

The fact that he was still left breathing was only a matter of luck.

CHAPTER NINETEEN

ELLA
HONEST

Honest: Free of deceit.

I should have seen the signs, been aware of when some-one was taking advantage of me. I shook my head at the thought. He didn't take advantage of me. He was curious as to why I was searching for him and I practically threw myself at him.

I still didn't have my answers and if I was honest with myself, I wasn't seeking the truth. I was seeking revenge.

I rubbed the back of my hand over my nose as I thought of my doll my mother had made me. It was my only connection to her and it was gone, possibly forever.

I couldn't go to my apartment or to work, knowing now that Maric is close to Rellik. As a person who prided herself on being a loner, I'd never felt this alone in my entire life. It was a dull aching in my chest, the world closing in on me. I was going to break down. Focusing on righting the wrongs of my past had always kept me going but I'd hit a wall.

Maybe it was time to accept that those who'd hurt me were going to get away with it, moving on to new victims. But Rellik was a different kind of animal. I pretended I was a strong, a means of self-preservation, but Rellik was the real deal. He was a beast and willing to do what beasts do. It terrified me. I'd wanted to meet him on my own terms, to know he could be trusted.

I slipped into the back corner of the library where computers lined the wall. I sat down at the one in the corner, to allow myself some privacy if anyone else showed, but most people had access to the internet at home so I was usually left to myself.

I pulled up the search page and typed in Silver Lake Hospital. There were endless pages for the facility.

"You're not going to find patient information on the internet," Rellik's voice in my ear caused me to jump. I spun around, my eyes scanning the empty room.

"You forgot your shoes." He glanced down at my bare feet as he held up a pair of my sandals.

"I left in a hurry."

"So you did." He tossed the shoes on the ground, the sound echoing in the quiet space.

"You want me to thank you?" I snapped as I grabbed the shoes and strapped them on my feet. He laughed, shaking his head in frustration.

"Last night was all the thanks I need."

I narrowed my eyes as he smirked.

"Fuck you."

"We did that already. I just want to talk." He tilted his head, eyebrow raised as he waited for me to decide what I wanted. "Come on, Ella. I'm trying to be nice here."

"It takes a lot for effort for you, doesn't it?"

"At the moment, yes." He rubbed his hand along his jaw, clearly losing his patience. "You know I'm not going to hurt you. If you thought so you would have screamed by now."

I knew if he didn't care, had no feelings he would have hurt me last night, instead he forced himself to be easy on me, even when I didn't want him to be. Rellik was raw and unfiltered, he acted on impulse but that didn't mean he was a bad person. He wasn't going to do anything to me, and that included causing a scene in public, just like in the parking lot.

"I'm sorry I threatened you."

"You're not forgiven."

"Don't you have something to say to me?"

"No."

"You don't want to apologize for pulling a gun on me?"

"I'm leaving." I walked around him, keeping my eyes ahead as made my way to the door. I could hear his footsteps behind me but I didn't quicken my pace. I knew I needed him but trusting him or anyone was too hard for me to do. I was stubborn and didn't like that he always had the upper hand.

Stepping outside, I was thankful for the cloud coverage that cloaked the world in an eerie grey. As much as I was trying to avoid spilling the truth to Ryder, I couldn't deny that I felt safer knowing he was behind me.

I walked slowly as his SUV crept beside me with his windows down. I refused to look at him. For once the heat wasn't oppressive and I actually enjoyed being able to gather my thoughts and figure out where I was going to go from here with what I needed to do. A few sporadic drops landed on me and I pretended not to notice.

"You're acting like a child," Ryder called out, not bothering to hide the irritation in his voice.

"Better than what *you're* acting like." I bit my lip to hide my smirk.

"And what's that, Ella?" His voice rose as if he was actually being playful, something I wasn't entirely sure he was capable of.

I couldn't help but glance over at him, my irritation evaporating. He had a way of making me forget. "You're a dick."

"You want my dick?" His voice carried and I ducked my head in embarrassment, not certain if anyone else was around.

I began to walk faster and he had to pass another car to stay beside me.

"Come on, Ella. You can do better than that."

"I could always do this," I slipped between two buildings and I heard him shout a curse and the engine accelerate behind me as he hurried to come around the block. I waited for the engine sound to fade into the distance before slipping back out the way I'd come and walking back in the direction of the library, the raindrops falling heavy now.

I knew I was poking a bear and part of me enjoyed knowing that as angry as I made Ryder, he held back. It was a twisted feeling but not one I'd experienced before. The men who'd come before him in my life didn't think twice about hurting me. There was a safety in this feeling and I needed to know he wouldn't give up on me like others had.

I continued by the library and hurried down Chester Avenue my eyes darting behind me whenever I'd heard a vehicle approach, unable to breathe until it past me by.

I'd almost made it to Langley Park when a pair of headlights blinded me and the vehicle rolled to a stop just a few feet away. I hesitated before slowly approaching it. The driver door opened and Ryder stepped out into the street, rain beating down on him and he looked like he was ready for a foot chase if necessary.

"You don't take a hint," I called out but his expression didn't soften and I knew I may have gone too far.

"Get in the fucking car, Ella."

"Since you asked so nicely." I started to walk by the vehicle and he moved behind it to cut me off at the rear end. Grabbing my shoulders he pressed me against the back of the SUV. I couldn't help but fixate on the drop of water that ran over his lower lip. I wanted to lick it off him, making it very hard to maintain my anger. But Ryder had a way to bring it out in people and he didn't waste a moment.

"Get in the fucking car. You're going to give me answers."

"And if I say no?"

He smirked, dimples settled into his tanned cheeks as he leaned closer, his eyes falling to my lips before raising them again. "You didn't say no last night."

Just like that I melted and I knew he saw it because the air around us seemed to change, electric-charged and begging for that connection.

He lowered his voice and I knew he was struggling not to let the sexual attraction between us cloud his judgment. "Come with me, Ella." The way he spoke, his words sounding explicit even when I knew it wasn't what he meant. I sucked in a ragged breath, feeling like I couldn't get enough air in my lungs, the oxygen supply to my brain being cut short. Flashes of my legs wrapped around his hips and our bodies moved together filled my thoughts. He leaned closer, inhaling the scent of my hair before whispering into my ear. "I could always make you."

My lips parted but I couldn't form a response as he pulled back, his mouth hovering over mine, our breathing shallow and lost in the moment. His hand left my shoulder and he slammed his palm against the damp window next to my head, snapping himself out of the moment. I startled but I knew his anger was directed inward. "Get in the fucking car." His tone was harsh and unlike anything he was in the bed with me last night.

"Make me," my childish tone made me cringe but he was so incredibly frustrating I couldn't help myself.

His mouth twisted in a half smile as grabbed my waist, bending over so he could lift me onto his shoulder.

"You fucking, asshole! Put me down!"

He walked to the passenger side of the car, ignoring my fists that pounded against his back. "I asked you nicely."

"Pfft. That's what you consider nice?" I snapped as he opened the door and lowered me to my feet, caging me between him and the seat.

"Get in." He stepped forward, pressing his body against mine. I had no choice but to sit down or let my brain turn to mush again just from being in such close proximity to him.

"Dick," I muttered under my breath as he closed the door, laughing. Jogging around the front of the vehicle, he got in, running his hand over his wet hair and sending water droplets sprinkling around him.

"Beautiful day." The engine roared to life with the push of a button and we pulled out, driving quickly through the wet seats. "Put on your seatbelt. Can never be too safe."

I scowled but pulled the belt across my lap and clicked it into place. "I want my things back."

"They're yours. I just want some answers."

I tried to ignore the tightening in my chest. There were certain things I never spoke about. Certain memories I didn't want to relive.

Ryder pulled out his phone and called the hotel, extending his stay for another night.

"I didn't realize you were leaving today."

His eyes went to the rearview mirror and back to the road. "I was going to go visit my mother. I have some business to take care of back home."

"Oh." We pulled into the parking lot and I got out of the car, looking out over the parking lot as I waited for Ryder. He walked by me and continued toward his room. "Is my stuff inside?" I called after him but he didn't respond. I followed, hating that I knew this was going to get worse before it got better.

He unlocked the door, leaving it open behind him. I scanned the room, noticing all of the belongings were gone. "Where are my bags?" I crossed my arms over my chest as Ryder walked back to me, reaching over my shoulder and shoving the door closed.

"I can't play this game with you anymore. It's fucking up my head, Ella."

"I'm not playing a game, Ryder. I want my things."

He reached forward and I took a step back, pressing myself against the door. "If you touch me I'll scream."

"If I touch you, you'll scream… and moan… and beg. I'm not going to fucking hurt you. Whoever has fucked up your head, Ella, I'm not them. I just need answers."

"I don't have any." I reached behind me, pulling open the door, glaring as I slipped back outside. I walked quickly across the lot the band's SUV and yanked open the back door. Inside was Ryder's duffle back and my bags. I put my book bag on my shoulders and turned to leave, shrieking when I almost collided with Ryder's chest.

"Get out of my way." I shoved against his chest and began to walk toward the overhang to get out of the rain.

CHAPTER TWENTY

RELLIK
BOND

Bond: a force or feeling that unites people; a common emotion or interest.

"The call you'd made from my room, who was that?" She spun around, damp hair clinging to her face, as if she didn't expect me to know that information.

"You forgot about that, huh? The room was registered to me, I can find out all of that information. You might want to remember that next time you scam someone."

"I wasn't scamming you," she yelled back angrily. "I had called someone from my work to let her know I was okay. That's it."

"Careful, Ella, you're not thinking your lies through. I already called the number."

"No." Her head shook and her eyes widened.

I nodded as my tongue swept across my lower lip, wiping away the dampness of the rain.

"You wouldn't have done that."

I cocked my head to the side and smirked as my eyes narrowed. "Are you sure about that? I think you'd be surprised at the things I would do."

"Oh, God." Her hand went to her stomach.

"There's no God here." I stepped closer, stopping within arm's reach of her. She looked up, eyes sad and searching mine. "He turned his back on me a long time ago."

"You really are crazy." Her eyes narrowed as they searched mine, desperately hoping it was all a sick, twisted joke.

"That hurts. You violated my privacy first, Ella. Of course, I guess this makes us even."

"What did you tell him? What did you say?"

"Who is he?"

"What did you do?" The absolute terror in her eyes was unlike anything I'd seen before.

I could see the wheels spinning in her head. She shoved her hand into her purse and let it fall to the ground as she held her gun toward me again. Newspaper clippings scattered on the ground around us. I bend down and picked one of the damp papers up with Katie's face on it. I stood up, eyeing Ella as hate pumped through me.

"I hope you remember what I told you. If you're going to aim that gun at me, you better pull the fucking trigger." Her hand shook as I stepped forward, pressing it against my chest. "Pull the trigger, Ella." I stepped forward again, causing her elbow to bend. "Pull it."

"I'll do it. I'll do it this time." She shook her head but I could see the indecision in her eyes.

"PULL THE FUCKING TRIGGER!"

And.

She.

Did.

The click of metal against metal was deafening in our heated state. The look of confusion on her face, priceless as the weapon failed to discharge. I smirked, not out of cockiness, but pride that she finally found the guts to stand up for herself. But it meant nothing. Her weapon was empty, like my heart that she so desperately wanted to quiet.

"No," She looked down at the weapon as if it would give her answers.

"That's unfortunate." I sighed as I grabbed the gun and tossed it to the ground. I'd underestimated her. She was a fighter. But she picked the wrong side.

"Now tell me who you called from the hotel room."

Her whole body seemed to vibrate with fear as her eyes darted around anywhere but landing on mine.

"You have no idea what you've done."

"Tell me something I don't know." My patience was wearing thin.

"You don't understand," She looked down at her shaking hands. I placed my fingers under her chin, tilting her gaze up to meet mine.

"Then fucking explain it to me, Ella. Give me a chance to help you or I am walking away."

"You'd still help me?" Her wide, emerald eyes searched mine for the truth. "Why?"

"As much as I want to hate you right now, you helped me move on from something that has been killing me for years. I owe you for that but make no mistake, when that debt is paid I want you gone."

Her bottom lip quivered and I had to look away. I didn't want to hurt her and I had to resist the urge to comfort her.

As much as I wanted to know what brought her into my life, I was dying to find out who had her so scared.

"I understand," she whispered with a sniffle.

"Then you better start talking."

She motioned with her chin towards the overhang of the building and I followed her to get out of the rain. Her hair was dripping wet down over her shirt that now clung to her curves.

She was good at appearing fragile and it was hard to separate the image she portrayed from the reality of the situation.

"I'm sorry."

"Don't. I'm not asking for more of your lies. Just tell me the truth."

With a heavy sigh her shoulders fell. "I've been looking for you."

"Stalker?" I shook my head. "Too simple. You can do better than that."

Her eyes met mine, glaring. "I'm not a stalker. I didn't know who you were at first. You wouldn't even tell me your real name. My name is Mikaella Martin, Ella is my nickname. When I was little my mom left me with my grandma. She said it was only temporary and she was trying to protect me from something. She never came back and my grandma died shortly after and I have had no one."

"Life is rarely fair. I'm still not seeing where I fit into all of this."

"No one ever told me why my mom was scared for my safety. It took years of digging and research to even find out what had happened to her."

"What happened?" I shoved my hands in my pockets, struggling to see where all of this was going.

"She's dead. At least I think she's dead. Murdered. I can't prove it."

"And you thought I'd understand? Losing a parent gave us some common ground?"

"No. Katie."

"Don't you dare talk about Katie." I struggled to contain my anger but Ella was twisting a knife into my heart.

"I don't want to bond with you over losing someone. Our bond *is* Katie." Her eyes were pleading with me to understand but if she thought looking like Katie was going to help her cause she was sadly fucking mistaken.

"Katie killed herself. She wasn't murdered. You have one minute to explain what the fuck you're talking about or I swear to fucking God, I'll call the number and lead whoever it is you're running from to your fucking door."

"You wouldn't." She left the cover of the porch as she struggled to collect her thoughts.

"You have no idea what I'm capable of, Ella."

I followed Ella from under the cover of the hotel back into the downpour. She stood with her back to me only a few feet away.

"What is it you're not telling me," I yelled over the sound of the rain. She shook her head and looked toward the ground.

"I can't," her voice trailed off as her shoulders shook under her sobs.

"God damn it, Ella!"

I waited for her to respond but she remained silent. Wiping my hand over my wet face, I brushed away the drops that clung to my skin. "I saw the look on your face when you mentioned the picture." I began to pace, struggling to keep my anger under control. "You knew her. Who are you, a cousin or something?"

"No."

"You're fucking *lying* to me." I couldn't calm my thoughts, I was clinging desperately to my last thread of sanity.

"I didn't know her. I couldn't have."

"Why is that?" I stepped closer, the energy in my body causing me to shift my weight from foot to foot. The anticipation of the truth was rushing through my veins like a high. If you could over-dose on pain I would gladly welcome the emptiness of the end over the not knowing.

With a deep breath she closed her eyes and shook her head, her dampened hair falling over her pained face. She was struggling with her own demons and part of me felt drawn to her because of that.

"Because she had already died before the Alexander's adopted me."

My body stilled, frozen as the words that she had spoken washed over me. I hadn't felt fear like this since the night Katie died. All these years I'd struggled to move on and the Alexander's simply replaced Katie like a fucking family pet.

"What the fuck did you just say?" Grabbing her shoulders with each hand I held her in front of me, afraid she would run from her own past that she had struggled to keep a secret.

"You aren't the only one who saw Katie when they looked at me." Her eyes met mine, pleading for understanding. She looked as though she was going to be physically ill.

"And Bryce?" Squeezing my eyes closed, I braced for the harsh truth that leaving Bryce alive that day I'd kicked his ass had not only taken Katie's life but destroyed Ella's.

"I've read the articles. They suspected sexual assault but with the rain there was little evidence. Not enough to tie you to it… or anyone else."

"Ella," I clutched my chest, the crippling pain too much to endure. Bryce hadn't been successful in his attack on Katie but it was more than apparent something had happened. She wouldn't have ended her life otherwise. Regardless of what anyone else thought, I would have *never* hurt Katie.

She nodded as a sob escaped her. "I *know* it wasn't you." Her body lurched forward as she began to cry, confirming what I'd known all along. I'd wished I'd left the bullets in the gun, the sweet pain of death would have been fractional compared to the torture that was unleashed with her words.

"I'm so sorry." I couldn't fathom the idea of Bryce's cycle of abuse continuing. My eyes searched hers as I struggled to ask her the questions I didn't want to know the answers to. I pulled her against my chest, squeezing her tightly, trying to absorb her cries, take her pain as my own. My fingers clutched her hair as I held her cheek against my heart. "This is all my fault. I should have fucking killed him eight years ago."

She shook her head and pulled back fractionally from my chest, her eyes swimming and red making the green even more vibrant. "It's not too late."

CHAPTER TWENTY-ONE

ELLA
EVIDENCE

Evidence: The available body of facts or information indicating whether a belief or proposition is true or valid.

For the first time I was able to look him in the eye and not feel shame or regret. We saw each other now for exactly who we were, without the lies and masks in place. No one suffered through the things we'd been through and came out the other side with a clean hands. I needed closure, to be able to sleep again at night without the monsters plaguing my nightmares. I needed a magic shield and that was Ryder.

"I have more than enough evidence to prove what kind of monster he is, but I need your help first."

"What is it you need me to do, sweetheart?"

"Right now, just don't let me go."

He pulled me back against him, squeezing me painfully tight as I held my breath, hoping he would agree once he knew what I needed from him. This was the first time I'd confessed to anyone what I'd endured and to know that he believed me, made me feel closer to him then I'd ever been to anyone in my life. But there were more confessions to be made. My past was much darker.

"This is all my fault, Ella. Had I…" His voice trailed off, his muscles growing tense against me. "I'll do whatever it is you need."

I let my eyes fall closed, reveling in his compassion as the rain washed away our secrets, baptizing us in our new commitment for righting the wrongs.

He pressed his lips to the top of my head. "Anyone who hurt you will regret it. I promise." The coldness and conviction in his voice sent a chill down my spine, but I'd never felt safer. "I promise, Ella."

I was tired of running from my past, but facing it was going to be the hardest thing I'd ever done. Rellik was struggling to hold it together as it was, and facing Bryce may break the final thread of sanity he'd been clinging to. But I needed his help and in return I'd give him the answers he'd been seeking since he was sixteen.

"Let's get you out of the rain." He ran his hand over my back, noticing the chill caused by his words. I tucked my damp hair behind my ears as I bent down to pick up the scattered contents of my purse, ruined from the weather.

I shoved them back in my bag as Rellik unlocked the door to the room and stepped aside for me to enter. My mind immediately went to the last night we'd spent together, but what we did paled in comparison to the intimate moment we'd just shared.

He closed the door behind us, the sound of the lock causing me to jump. "Let me get you some dry clothes."

He walked around me to his bag on the dresser, dripping onto the carpet as he dug through the contents.

I gripped my t-shirt and pulled it over my head, shaking my hair as it clung to my skin. Rellik's eyes met mine before drifting over my chest.

My fingers went to the button of my jeans, undoing them and pulling the zipper down before sliding them down my legs. I stood in front of him in only damp, purple panties, completely exposed for the first time in my life.

"Ella," his voice laced with pain as he shook his head fractionally, gripping the bag tightly in his fists.

"Don't do that. Don't look at me with pity."

"You think I *pity* you? You're one of the strongest fucking women I've ever met. I don't deserve to get to touch you. Not after what happened to you."

"You're the only person I *want* to touch me."

"You don't mean that." He looked to the ground, the muscles jumping over his jaw, doubt plaguing him.

"Ryder, all I want right now is for you to fuck me like you've never wanted anyone more." I was putting myself out on a limb, and fear of rejection caused my nerves to stand on end, the seconds it took him to think over what I said agonizing. "Please."

"That's easy, sweetheart." He pulled his wet shirt over his head and tossed it on the ground, drops of water running down the ridges of his abdomen and disappearing into the waist of his boxers. Before he could change his mind I stepped in front of him, my fingers quickly undoing the button of his jeans and sliding the zipper over his hardening cock.

"Please, don't be gentle with me," I whispered, my words breathier than I intended, but their meaning was not lost as his fingers wrapped around my ribs and he pressed me hard against the wall, the evidence of how much he wanted me against my stomach.

"Are you sure this is what you want, darling?" I could tell he was struggling to keep control over himself, but all I wanted was for him to let go and take me as if I wasn't a victim. I knew he had been holding himself back for years, pretending to not care. But I needed him to prove to me now that he does. No more bullshit. No more hiding.

"I've never wanted *anyone* more, Ryder."

"I'd take it all away if I could."

"It's not your fault. What happened to her… to me… not your fault."

His gaze went from my eyes to lips and I knew that he saw me now, the way I saw him. It was real. He saw me as Ella. The lies, the guilt all fell away in this moment and we were free to share our pain. His hips pressed hard against mine and I pushed back with equal force, determined to prove I wouldn't break under his touch.

I pressed my lips against his, tentative at first, begging for the desire I knew he felt. He groaned, as my lips parted and I ran the tip of my tongue over his lower lip. My wet chest slid against his causing my nipples to harden as he bit down gently on my lower lip, tugging at it with a wicked grin.

I looped my arms around his neck and pulled him back against me so I could continue our kiss. Slipping his hand between us, he freed himself from his boxers and pressed the head of his cock against my clit.

"Don't tease me," I moaned, rocking my hips forward. He slid my panties to the side as he slid his head lower, to my entrance.

"I don't want to be gentle."

"I want you any way I can have you." I giggled as he lifted me from my feet, my legs wrapping around his waist. My laughter died in my throat as he began to enter me, his forehead pressed against mine. We shared the same air, the same secrets. It was all so real, so raw. It was painful, but not physically. Unravelling in his arms, his body rocked against mine. He fisted his hand in my hair holding my mouth against his as he turned and gently laid me on the bed.

"Any way?" His eyebrow cocked as he took his boxers completely off. "Roll over, sweetheart."

I nervously rolled onto my stomach. Rellik's fingers looped around my panties and slowly began to drag them down my legs as he pressed his lips against my right ass cheek, his facial hair tickling me and causing me to laugh. He spread my legs apart slightly so he could kneel behind me as he gripped my hips and pulled me up on my knees.

He placed his palm in the center of my back and pressed against me until I lowered from my hands to my elbows.

"God you're fucking beautiful." His hand was on the small of my back as his other gripped his cock that was now pressed against my entrance. Painfully slow he entered me, hissing between his teeth when his was completely inside of me.

My fingers tangled in the sheets, gripping them as he withdrew until only his head was inside of me and slammed back into me hard. I moaned as he gripped my hips, his fingers bruising my flesh as he held me in place. The sounds emanating from his throat were so fucking sexy and I wished I could see what we looked like together right now.

I began to push back against him, meeting his thrusts eagerly as my release began to build. His hand slid over now sweat soaked skin as he massaged my clit, his chest against my back. I began to tighten around him in waves of pleasure, but he pulled out before I finished, grabbing my shoulder and flipping me onto my back.

"I want to watch you come," He growled as he climbed on top of me and slid back inside of me. I let my eyes dance over his stomach muscles, as the pulled and tightened with each thrust.

"Oh, God," I moaned as my orgasm began to build again.

"Look at me."

I opened my eyes as pleasure ripped through me. "Ryder," I panted as his mouth found mine, hard and the warmth of his own release filled me.

We spent the rest of the day fucking away every bad memory and secret we shared, both desperate to take back control of our lives.

Chapter Twenty-Two

RELLIK
RESIST

Resist: Withstand the action or effect of.

I laid awake all night, watching Ella sleep. I struggled to resist the urge to wake her as she had a nightmare, her face twisted in pain. I was dying to know what was going on inside that beautiful head of hers.

She stirred and I held my breath, watching her eyes flutter open and the corners of her lips turn up into a smile when she saw me.

"How long have you been looking at me?" She pushed the hair from her face and bowed her back toward me as she stretched.

"A few hours."

"I'm not sure if that's really sweet or fucking creepy."

"If you only knew the dirty thoughts I was thinking."

"Only you could make that sound sexy." I studied her face as her smile faded. "What?"

"You're going to have to tell me what it is you need help with sooner or later."

She sat up, clutching the sheet over her bare chest.

"It's too early for this, Ryder."

I reached out, gripping the ends of her hair that cascaded down her bare back and twisted the ends around my finger before letting it fall free. "Ella, there is nothing you can say that will change anything. I promised to help you. I keep my promises."

"Those newspaper articles." She glanced over her shoulder at me and I nodded. "The ones about the Dream Killer? I think I know who he is."

I pushed myself up to sit next to her. "Who?"

"My father." Her eyes searched mine, desperate for me to believe her.

"What?"

"I know this sounds crazy, but it makes sense. If you read the articles. All of the bodies found have a dream catcher somewhere near them. Before I went to live with my grandma, I always had to have a dream catcher above my bed. I called it my magic shield because it protected me from my nightmares about someone hiding in my closet."

"Ella," I ran my hand over my jaw as I shook my head.

"You don't believe me. I fucking knew you wouldn't believe me."

"It's not that. It's just… dream catchers are a common item. It's normal for kids to have them in their room."

"Was it normal to hear noises coming from my parent's closet, and being brave enough to open the door to find a man bound and gagged inside?"

"Momma," I screamed, unable to move as I stared into the desperate eyes of a man, tied to a chair that laid on its side. He was struggling to free his hands. Even gagged, I could tell he wanted my help.

"Get back to bed, Mikaella," my father's voice boomed from behind me as the closet door was pushed closed and he sank down to eye level. "You know there are monsters in the closet who hurt little girls who don't go to sleep. It's past your bedtime." He ran his large hand over my hair with a smile.

"Momma said monsters aren't real."

He clenched his jaw, his tone turning harsh. "Your momma's a fucking liar. Get to bed. Daddy's gonna take care of this one so he can't hurt you." He stood, towering over me with his large six foot frame. I nodded and ran off to bed, unable to calm my erratic breathing. I sat on my bed, covers pulled up to my neck as I stared at my closet door, terrified that someone was inside.

"What the fuck, Ella?"

"Doesn't sound so crazy now, does it?"

"Actually, now it sounds really fucking crazy, but I understand why you think it's your father. What is it you want me to do?"

"I need to know if he killed my mother."

"You want me to confront a man who ties up people and shoves them in closets?"

"I want you to kill him."

CHAPTER TWENTY-THREE

ELLA
SPECIAL

**Special: Better, greater or otherwise
different from what is usual.**

"You want me to *kill* your father?" When Ryder repeated my words back to me I knew I was losing my mind. I had just asked him to commit murder and to be honest, I meant it.

"I know you don't know me and I know I'm asking a lot." I shook my head, a nervous laugh escaping me. "I've fucking lost it."

"Stop." He tucked my hair behind my ear, his fingertips trailing down my cheek. "I feel like we know each other better than anyone. I know this isn't something you'd say to anyone else."

"I will tell you what I know about Bryce. You can walk away. You don't have to do this just to get information."

"Jesus Christ, Ella! I'm not helping you for Bryce. I'm doing it for *you*. Nothing's changed." His fingers gripped my chin, forcing me not to look away. "Nothing."

I lurched forward, my lips pressing against his painfully hard. His hands slid down my back, gripping my bare ass as he guided me only his lap. The sheet pulled free from my body as he lowered me onto his cock. My nails dug into the back of his neck as I sank down his length. Desperate to be closer to him.

I rocked my hips, riding him as his lips found my neck, sucking and licking. His hands were all over my body, relishing every curve. "I love watching you fuck me," He groaned as he pulled my nipple between his teeth.

It didn't matter how I felt about myself, Ryder had a way of making every flaw feel beautiful. I wondered if he made other women feel that way. The thought made my stomach sink and I ducked my head.

"Hey?" His fingers went under my chin and our bodies stilled as he raised my face, forcing me to look at him. "What's wrong?" Our bodies stilled as his eyes searched mine.

"You… you make me feel so… special."

"You don't think you are?"

"It's not that." I shrugged but that was part of the problem.

"Ella."

I ducked my head just as a tear fell but I knew had seen it. He pulled me against his chest, holding me while I broke down until my sobs quieted and my body stilled. Carefully, he rolled us over and positioned himself between my legs. His fingers ran over my cheek as he wiped away my tears and very slowly entered me. I'd never made love before, never knew what loving a man could feel like, but with Ryder I could easily slip inside of that fantasy.

He kissed me tenderly as he whispered my name against my lips, making me feel like I was the only woman in the world.

"You're so beautiful," he mumbled as my hips rolled against his. "So perfect."

I was hungry now for his kisses but he controlled the pace. There was a reason people like us chose hard and rough. Emotionally connecting with someone else wasn't what we were looking for, and avoided at all costs. That's how you kept from getting hurt.

I wrapped my arms around him and held his body tight against mine, needing to be as close as possible to him.

"You are special, Ella." My body pulsed around him as he grew even harder. "You," his eyes locked onto mine. "Are one of a kind."

He saw me. I wasn't the girl who looked like Katie. He was doing this for me. I came undone whispering his name against his lips. His body tensed as he followed, panting my name.

Chapter Twenty-Four

RELLIK

Hurt: Cause physical pain or injury.

Ella rolled away from me and I pulled her back against my chest, wrapping my arms tightly around her waist. "I'd never done that before."

I pressed my lips against her bare shoulder. "Neither have I. I'm glad I was your first."

She snuggled in tighter against me, her body fitting against mine like she was made to be there.

"I want you to think about what you asked me to do, Ella. I don't want you to regret it later and hate me for it."

"This isn't something I asked from you on a whim. I would do it myself if I knew I could."

"You don't have to."

She fell silent and I struggled to ask her the question that was on my mind since she told me about her father. "Did he *hurt* you? Touch you?"

She shook her head and wiped her hand under her eye. "No. he was a different kind of monster."

I pressed my lips against her temple and she sighed. "And your mother?"

"I don't think she ran from him. I think she gave herself to him so he wouldn't come looking and find me."

"Jesus, Ella."

"The gun. I want you to use the gun."

"I can't shoot your dad with your weapon. They can trace it back to you with ballistics."

"It's not my gun."

I propped myself up on my elbow and looked down at her. She rolled onto her back, a small smile playing on her lips. "A few months ago I saw Coach at a grocery store. I waited for him to go inside and when he did I searched his glove box. I found his new address and that gun." She shrugged. "Kill two birds with one stone."

"You're amazing." I sat up, grabbing her hands and pulling her from the bed. "What are we waiting for?"

I quickly called Trigger and explained to him that I needed any information he could find on Ella's mother and he agreed not to mention it to Phantom.

CHAPTER TWENTY-FIVE

RELLIK
SACRIFICE (2)

**Sacrifice: destruction or surrender of
something for the sake of something else.**

Looking out at the rundown house, white paint peeling
to reveal old warped rotten wood, my stomach turned.
Inside would hold unspeakable secrets of torture and
death. It was the physical manifestation of the evil that
dwelled inside of it. I gripped Ella's hand, her eyes meeting
mine. There was sadness in her gaze but no uncertainty.

"You don't have to be here for this." I rubbed my
thumb against the back of her hand as she stared at the
dilapidated building.

"I need answers."

I swallowed hard as I climbed the broken front steps
and pulled open the screen door that hung by one hinge.
It squeaked loudly and a man yelled from somewhere
inside, followed by a loud hacking cough. He pulled open
the front door and narrowed his eyes. I looked him over
him in his dirty jeans stained will motor oil and dirty,
white cotton shirt and my stomach rolled at the smell

of mildew that wafted off him. I tugged the bill of my worn out White Sox hat lower. He was much older than I'd expected.

"What?" he snapped. I glanced around him at the woman who stood behind him, shirt torn, bone-thin and covered in bruises. The same dead look in my eyes reflected in hers. She had suffered, seen things no one should.

His eyes went to Ella and they lit up in recognition. "Mikaella?" He took a step forward and I stepped to my right to get between them. His eyes narrowed as he looked me over.

"You best get out of my way before I move you myself."

"I wouldn't make threats if I were you."

His gaze went back to Ella and I knew he was trying to intimidate her to get his way.

"Ella is looking for her mother."

His laughter caused my eye to twitch. I wouldn't have spent another God damn second talking to this asshole, but she needed answers.

"Haven't seen that dumb bitch in years."

"We just want to know where she is."

He looked me over suspiciously before shaking his head. "I already told you no. Now leave." He slammed the door and I sighed as I retreated down the stairs, glancing over my shoulder at the dilapidated house as he yelled obscenities inside, presumably at the woman. It was hard to walk away knowing just what went on in places like this, but I had no other choice.

It was times like these that I was thankful I felt empty inside because the guilt alone would have killed me. I pulled a cell phone from my pocket and dialed Trigger's number. He was the only one of the guys that knew I still had Ella around. It rang twice before he picked up and the music in the background made it impossible to hear him.

"No luck."

"None on this end either." If there was an electronic trail Trig would have found it. Ella's mom had vanished with no trace.

"I guess it's plan B then."

There was a pregnant pause before the line went dead and I handed my phone my phone to Ella, mumbling obscenities under my breath. "Go wait in the car. If he has answers, I will find them out for you."

"I'll never know what happened to her."

"He'll talk. Trust me." I pressed my lips against her forehead before taking a step back. She nodded and reluctantly got into the passenger side of the SUV.

I walked up the steps, not bothering to knock as I opened the front door causing it to bang loudly off the wall behind it. The woman appeared, shaken as he froze, wide eyed.

"Does he hurt you?" I asked just as the old man made his way down the steps.

"What the hell are you doing here? This is private property, you son of a bitch!" He growled. I ignored him and returned my gaze to the woman.

"Answer me truthfully and I'll make sure he never hurts you again."

She looked to the man and back to me, hopeful. "Yes," she whispered and I gestured to the door behind me with a nod. "Go. Run. Find someone to call the police. Forget you saw me." I knew it would take her a few minutes at least to get to the next property.

"The police?" the old man sneered. "What are they going to do?"

"Identify your body," I snapped back to him as she ran around me and out the front door. The man's eyes grew wide and he retreated up a step.

"You can't just come in here and threaten me. Do you have any idea who I am? Didn't Mikaella tell you?"

I put my foot on the first step and he stumbled backwards climbing higher. Ella and I both knew her mother was long dead. She was never going to get her answers, but at least I can make sure he can never hurt her again.

"Yeah. She told me who you are. You want to know who I am?" I asked as I moved slowly towards him. "I expected a monster, a challenge. You're just a weak old man."

"That girl never did know how to listen. Just another dumb bitch like her mother." He was still yelling but his voice wavered and I knew he was afraid. Funny how the biggest bullies only liked to pick on the small and fragile who can't defend themselves. "You want that girl? She's all yours. I'm sure she hasn't gotten far yet. I won't even charge you."

My stomach sank and the world around me went black. Anger flooded me and before I could stop myself I was over top of the man, swinging wildly. His wrinkled papery skin busted and bled under my fists. I felt the bones in his nose crumble under my knuckles and he slipped, falling back onto the stairs with a grunt, moaning as he struggled to protect his face with his arms. I hit him again and the sound finally stopped and I was finally able to get myself back under control. I stood over him, my chest heaving as I struggled to calm my breathing. I didn't want it to be this easy. He deserved worse.

I reached into my pocket and pulled out a small green lighter and a cigarette from my pack. I lit it, blowing out the smoke toward him as he hacked. "Bad habit." I turned the cigarette in my hand as he struggled to push himself up. Putting my foot on his chest I shook my head and took another drag, causing the cherry to glow orange.

"What happened to Ella's mother?"

"I don't know." He shook his head and I smiled before pressing the cigarette against his cheek.

"I've heard some interesting stories about you," I raised my voice to be heard over his groans. "Ella told me all about the skeletons in your closet."

His eyes widened but he didn't speak.

"She just wants to know what happened to her mother." Taking another drag I flicked my ashes onto his shirt. "Fine." I bent over, poised to burn him again.

"She's dead." He waved his hands between us to keep me from hurting him again. I closed my eyes, knowing it was going to destroy Ella.

Most would look at him as a helpless old man, but I could see the darkness, in his eyes. I pulled the gun from the back of my jeans and squeezed the trigger, the echo of the shot deafening in the empty space.

I wiped my fingerprints from the gun with my shirt and dropped it beside his body as blood puddled on the steps underneath him. Even if I didn't find Bryce, Coach's gun being used as a murder weapon would draw them out like cockroaches.

I glanced around the silent house before hurrying down the steps and looking out the front door for anyone else. I dug my keys from my pocket and got into the SUV, slowly creeping down the dirt road so I wouldn't cause the dust to kick up.

"What did he say?" Ella's body was vibrating with anxiety. I couldn't even look at her.

"She's gone."

My gaze fell to my bloodied hands on the wheel, my body shaking with unspent energy. It wasn't enough. He had given up too quickly and it felt like I hadn't done justice for the nameless woman or Ella. He should have suffered for every unspeakable act he had committed, but he would play a vital role in a bigger plan that had been set in motion when I was only sixteen years old. Now I would get Bryce.

I wiped my hand over my face as I turned into an old abandoned gas station parking lot to gather my thoughts. I could hear sirens in the distance and adjusted the rear-view mirror to see a police car approaching and disappearing past me on the road. My eyes then focused on my own reflection, blood smeared over my eye and down my jaw. I took the hat off and tossed it on the passenger seat.

"Fuck," I grabbed my shirt and pulled it off, using it to rub my face clean and them my hands. Ella grabbed a bottle of water from the floor to make the shirt damp and scrubbed what had begun to dry to my skin.

I had been careless, my feelings for Ella clouding my judgment. I examined my knuckles for cuts or scrapes but my skin was flawless and I sighed with relief that I hadn't left any of my own blood behind. I glanced at my reflection again and only empty blue eyes stared back at me. I put the car in drive and pulled back onto the road and headed toward the hotel.

I waited for the lot to be empty before getting out, not wanting to be recognized by someone I knew. Luckily it was hot and the fact that I was shirtless wouldn't render me a second glance. I put on a pair of sunglasses and hurried to my room with the shirt and hat, my arm around Ella.

"Relax." I rubbed my hand over her arm to soothe her. She forced a smile and slowed her pace to not draw any attention to us.

When we got inside the room I fell back against the door, struggling to catch my breath. Ella's back was to me and I couldn't tell if she was on the verge of breaking down.

"Say something. Anything."

She turned to me, teary-eyed but smiling. "At least now I know."

"It's almost over."

I ran through the shower quickly, changing into a pair of dark wash jeans and my favorite black Doors shirt. The concert was in two hours and the guys were already doing sound checks over at Grayson's Spot. As I laced up my black Adidas sneakers breaking news of a murder came on the news.

I shook my head and grabbed my book bag and headed out to rehearsal which was only a few miles away.

Trigger looked up at me as I entered and shook his head before playing a few cords on his guitar.

"You're late," he said without looking back up at me.

"The cops had Roman Street blocked off for a fender bender."

"It's a dangerous world out there," He glanced up with a smirk as he continued to play.

We rehearsed for the next hour before eating pizza that we'd ordered from The Peddler. I was on edge, anxious to get back to Ella. I hated leaving her alone after what I'd just done. But I couldn't skip out on the gig or Phantom would no without a doubt who I'd been with. I couldn't have him stopping me from what I had to do.

We played to a packed house but I couldn't see anyone but Ella as I sang through our set. By the time our gig ended I told the guys I was heading off with some bar slut to her apartment so I could go back to Ella.

Ella was asleep, curled up in a ball in the center of the bed. I took off my clothing and crawled in behind her, wrapping my body around hers. She sighed contently in her sleep and I laid with her in my arms wide awake for hours.

CHAPTER TWENTY-SIX

ELLA

When I awoke, Ryder was already dressed and sitting on a chair, watching me.

"Get ready. We have something we need to do."

"What is it?" I yawned, stretching my back. "You could have woken me up."

"You looked so peaceful." His smile cause my cheeks to heat. I pushed from the bed and went to the bathroom to brush my teeth and get ready as quickly as possible. Ryder followed, leaning against the door frame and watching my in the mirror.

"I need to go get my car. I can't keep taking the Durango and leaving the guys stranded."

"Where's your car?" I spit into the sink and turned on the water to rinse my mouth.

"At my mom's house. She shouldn't be home at this time of day."

I wanted to ask him why he was trying to avoid his mother, but I knew he would tell me if that was information he wanted to share.

By the time I was finished getting ready, Ryder had already called a cab and it was outside waiting for us. He put our bags in the trunk and held open the door for me to slide into the back seat before getting in beside me.

He gave the driver the address and tapped his fingers to the beat of an unfamiliar song on arm rest as we made our way out of the city area and into Eddlebrook.

"That one." He pointed to a small ranch style beige house. After the paying the driver and grabbing our bags.

"Just wait right here." He said as we stepped inside. I stood in the entryway as he disappeared down the hall and through another door. After a few minutes I was growing impatient and desperately needed to use the bathroom. I walked down the hall and pushed open the door he had gone through.

"Wow, that's your car?" I stepped closer and Ryder spun around just as my eyes landed on the rearview mirror.

CHAPTER TWENTY-SEVEN

RELLIK
CONSEQUENCES

**Consequences: A result or effect
of an action or condition.**

I felt my chest tighten as she peered inside of the old
Barracuda, the memories flooding back like a tsunami.
Her eyes met mine and went back to the dream catcher
that hung from the rearview mirror. I watched as all of
the puzzle pieces snapped together in her mind.

"Say something." I could barely form the words, the
betrayal she felt palpable hanging thick and heavy in the
air between us.

"You knew. This whole time you *knew* it wasn't my
father."

"That doesn't make his crimes any less horrific,
Ella."

"But what does it make *you*?" She stepped back fractionally but it was enough for me to notice she was scared,
contemplating running. For the first time, someone was
looking at the real me, the murderous vengeful monster
who craved retribution. "You're the Dream Killer."

"Ella," her name rolled off my tongue, painfully, as if saying goodbye. "I promise you, I never hurt Katie." I took a step forward, my hands in front of me, palms facing her to let her know I wasn't a threat.

"Who *did* you hurt?" Her voice cracked under the fear and I wanted to kill myself for making her afraid. She had been through enough and the last thing I wanted was to hurt her. But I'd be lying to say I didn't enjoy what I did. Watching the light die out in the eyes of those I hated satisfied a deep primal need inside of me. It was as necessary as gasping for a breath of air, for the heart to pump blood.

"No one who didn't deserve it."

Her eyes swam, her finger pointed at me as she retreated further. "Don't. Don't you *dare.*"

"Please let me explain."

"You're just like my father," she choked out, a tear spilling over her lashes and rolling down her cheek.

"The father you asked me to *kill*?"

"It's not the same." Her body bowed at the waist and she was on the verge of becoming ill.

"Why isn't it? Ella, he was a bad man. I did what you asked of me. I *helped* you."

"No." she shook her head, begging to take back what we'd had together. "No."

"Please, just let me explain. Please." I couldn't fathom the betrayal she must have felt. She'd bared herself to me, shared her darkest secrets and I mascaraed as her hero. I was no better than the monsters in her closet, the monsters in her head.

"Jesus Christ, I'm such a fucking cliché. The girl with daddy issues." She laughed sardonically.

"That's not what this is. It's not who I am."

"Who *are* you, Ryder? Who the fuck are *you* because you're not the hero?"

"I'm your magic shield, Ella." We fit together so perfectly, bonded by dark pasts. She swallowed hard, nodding slightly as she visibly relaxed, understanding that our bond was special.

"I made a mistake. I was young and I did something that I could never have understood the consequences for." My hands dropped to my sides as I relived the horrible tragic nightmare of my father's death.

"Ryder, I'm with a customer."

"I figured out the chorus for Behind Blue Eyes." I was beyond excited at how my skills on the guitar had progressed, but my father blew me off, turning his attention back to the young blonde whose car my father had just replaced the front brakes on.

He put his hand on her shoulder to guide her out of the garage, his fingers lingering on her bare skin as she laughed flirtatiously. He leaned closer, whispering something in her ear and she smacked him playfully on the chest.

"Finish up that wheel, Ryder." He called behind him as they slipped outside into the darkness. I propped my guitar in the corner of the garage and went to the front passenger side of the car. I kicked the cotter key across the garage floor, muttering curse words under my breath as I bent down to finish securing the tire. I'd spent all day helping him replace the front breaks just to get a moment to show him what I'd learned.

The consequences of my anger didn't become relevant until a few days later when that tire flew off causing them to lose control and wreck.

"What did you do?"

My attention snapped back to Ella, her lips quivering as she struggled to understand.

"I killed my father."

Her hand went over her mouth as she gasped audibly.

"It was an accident and losing him destroyed my entire life." The only thing that kept me grounded was Katie, she was gravity, a force strong enough to help me suppress the anger inside of me.

"Was Katie an accident too?"

"I *never* hurt her. I… loved her. You have to believe me." Another blow, a stabbing pain directly in my heart. I wondered if that is how my victims felt. If the betrayal was worse than the actual mercy of death.

"Why? Why does it matter what I think of you?"

"Because I need you to know I wouldn't do anything to you. I could never hurt you."

"You *are* hurting me. I trusted you. I told you things I've never said to anyone."

I closed my eyes, struggling to silence the voices, the onslaught of memories. "I'm trying to *help* you, Ella."

"Bryce?" Her eyes widened, and I could see that she was hopeful he was dead, her heart disagreeing with her mind.

"A little hypocritical, don't you think?"

Her eyes went back to the dream catcher as she wrapped her arms around herself. "I don't know what to think." She shook her head, the wheels inside her mind spinning as she struggled to admit she was no different from me. I did what she couldn't, I ended the nightmares for her.

"It's not about right and wrong, Ella. I've never hurt anyone who didn't deserve it. I don't *need* to kill, I *want* to."

"Is that any better?"

"Some people are born this way, unable to control the urge. I was created, I became this on purpose. And it all lead to you. Don't you see that? You're the butterfly. You flapped your wings and the entire universe set us into motion. It was an unstoppable force. I became this for *you*, before I ever knew you existed."

"The butterfly effect," she mumbled under her breath.

"You never have to be scared again."

"My magic shield," she whispered and her eyes met mine. I walked toward her slowly, desperate to close the gap between us, to feel that electrical force that pulled us together before she knew what I really was.

"Bryce isn't dead." I swallowed back the rage that boiled inside of me whenever I thought of him. "What happens to him is up to you."

"What?"

"I'll walk away for you, Ella. Just please don't walk away from me."

"After what he did to Katie? After what he did," her voice trailed off.

"After what? Tell me. You don't have to carry around that pain by yourself."

She walked around me, blowing out a long breath as she sat down in the old kitchen chair in the corner of the garage.

CHAPTER TWENTY-EIGHT

ELLA
DESERVE

Deserve: Do something or have or show qualities worthy of reward or punishment.

"I moved in with the Alexander's when I was fifteen. At first it was... amazing. They treated me like they loved me before they even knew me. It didn't take long to figure out why."

I smiled nervously as Ryder clenched his jaw, struggling to keep the emotions from showing on his face.

"I wore her clothes, slept in her bed. Her picture, like the picture in your wallet, hung in my room."

"Christ," Ryder shook his head as he began to pace the floor.

"Bryce didn't live at home. *Home.*" The word sounded so wrong. Home was supposed to be a sanctuary, a place to feel safe in a dangerous world. "He started coming by several times a week. He was friendly."

Ryder sneered as he put his palms down on the hood of the old car, struggling to keep his composure. The clapping sound of his hands against the metal caused me to startle.

"Then he started coming by when my... when the adults would leave for work or to run errands. I tried to fight him off but he was twice my size. Sometimes I think he would let me get away just so he could chase me. He got some sort of sick thrill from my fear."

"You wear that dress just for me?" Bryce's eyes travelled up my legs as his hands ran over the growing bulge in his jeans.

"I hate these dresses. They were what she liked, not me." I took a few steps backwards to create some distance between us as I glanced down at the pale yellow eyelet dress.

"Want to know what I like?" He cocked his head to the side, a sickening smirk on his lips as he ran his tongue over his top row of teeth. My heart was racing and I wished I could lock Bryce away in my father's closet. But the monsters didn't always stay hidden away.

He lurched forward, grabbing my wrist painfully tight, laughing as I struggled against his grip.

"Fight me," he goaded as I pounded the side of my fist against his chest. "Fight me!" He grabbed my shoulder and shoved me backwards, hard. It felt like my tailbone had broken as I hit the wooden floor. My agonizing screams only making him want me more. We'd been doing this for months. I struggled to not fight him because I knew it was what he liked, but it only caused him to get more creative with his abuse. The latest cuts from the razor hadn't even healed as he hovered over me, digging his thumb into the wound.

I bit back my scream, my teeth digging into my lower lip until the taste of copper flooded my tongue. "Just kill me already and get it over with."

"I don't want to kill you, Katie."

"My name is not Katie!" *I untangled my hand from his shirt and slapped him as hard as I could across the face. His body stilled over me before his eyes met mine.*

"You stupid fucking bitch!" *His fist came down hard against my cheek, the back of my head slamming off the floor.*

My eyes closed for what felt like a fraction of a second and when I awoke, I was blinded my neon lighting, the low hum of the bulbs causing my head to ache.

"He raped you."

"More times than I can count."

Ryder crossed the garage and sank down in front of me, his hands on my knees. Raising his hand slowly, he wiped away a tear with the pad of his thumb. His other hand gripping me tightly as he struggled to keep his composure.

"The last time," I cleared my throat and shifted in my seat. "I woke up in a hospital, cuts all over my stomach and thighs. I didn't even recognize myself in a mirror for weeks."

His grip tightened on my knee and I placed my palm over it causing him to relax immediately.

"I was wrong." He pushed to his feet faster than before and paced the floor as he plotted. "I *need* to kill him, Ella." He stopped in front of me again and dipped down to eye level. "I *have* to make him suffer."

I swallowed hard, knowing my opinion could sway him, but I didn't have the strength to stop him because what was right, was to make him pay for the abuse I'd endured.

"He deserves it." I paused between each word making sure to annunciate them clearly, so he understood that we were on the same page.

"Tell me, Ella." His eyes searched mine, excited as if I told a child they could open their Christmas presents early. "Tell me you want me to *kill him*."

"I want you to kill him."

Sliding his hand into my hair he pulled me toward him, pressing his lips hard against my mine. The bond we shared running deeper than secrets. If I was the butterfly, he was the storm, the justice that would wash away my past so I could start again. We'd finish this together, heal each other.

CHAPTER TWENTY-NINE

RELLIK

Sanctuary: A place of refuge or safety.

"I want to take you somewhere." I stood, taking her hand and pulling her to her feet before motioning toward the car.

I needed Ella to see that I wasn't anything like her father, needed her to understand what brought us both to this point.

I drove us to the one place I swore I'd never go again.

It felt like I had never left that small wooded area where I ran for sanctuary and eventually found immeasurable heartbreak. The area looked like she had never stepped foot there, never whispered her secrets to me, never took her last breath amongst its roots. The blood had long absorbed into the earth and she was now a part of this place. If I closed my eyes I swore I could almost feel my heart start to quicken, like it had when we were together.

I fell to my knees, the damp grass soaking through my jeans. Could one really get closure if they didn't want to forget?

The rustling of footsteps jarred me from my morbid memories.

"Is this where it happened?" I glanced over my shoulder at Ella before looking back to the ground, struggling to convince myself that she was real, that life had given Katie back to me in.

"This is it. This is where I fell in love."

"Tell me what happened."

I closed my eyes, not knowing where to begin. "I don't like to talk about it."

Ella placed her hand on my shoulder, her thumb gently gliding back and forth against my shirt. "I want to understand what happened to me and I can't without her story."

"If you're looking for a reason, something that could have been changed, you're just going to drive yourself crazy."

"I just need to understand."

I swallowed hard, my throat dry as I struggled to come up with the words, to allow myself to slip wholly into the memories that tortured me. "Katie was there for me when I lost my father. She had no reason to be and had she not shown me kindness, she'd still be alive."

Ella sank down beside me and crossed her legs in front of her as I continued to stare off at the trees, letting my vision blur.

"We would come here, sneak out to see each other whenever we could."

"Why did you sneak around?"

Shrugging a picked up a leaf and began to pull it apart, separating the veins. "After my dad died I kind of lost it for a while. I got in a lot of fights. Katie was the only person who could calm me down."

"She was good for you."

"I was bad for her." Shaking my head I sank back on heels as I breathed in the smell of the trees.

"How long were you together?"

"Four years. We were sixteen when she…" I let my words die in my throat. "Katie was having trouble at home. Her step-brother wouldn't leave her alone. I got mad. I couldn't just let him get away with what he was doing to her. She begged me not to do anything."

"That doesn't mean you shouldn't have."

"Had I left him alone she'd still be alive."

"Had you left her alone he would have continued hurting her."

"Instead he hurt you." My eyes met hers, my chest tightening with regret.

"You couldn't have known. You can't blame yourself for what others have done."

"You blamed me."

"I blamed everyone. It didn't seem like I ever had a chance." We stared off in silence for a moment as I thought that over. Were we all just victims of fate, an unstable force?

"How did she do it? The papers didn't go into detail."

"Ella," I shook my head, my voice strained from the sudden flash of crimson that circled her body. "She slit her wrists."

"In the middle of the woods? She brought a knife all the way out here? Why wouldn't she go to your place?"

"This was *our* place. She texted me but my parents had taken my phone because of all the trouble I'd gotten into. The knife… the knife was my father's."

She looked at me with confusion as I ran my hand over my hair and blew out a heavy breath. "I kept it here. It was one of the few things I had of his. When my step-dad moved in he took over the house. It felt like my dad never existed. I didn't want it to become his. It was mine." My eyes darted to the old oak tree, with the large crescent hole at its base. "My box." I pushed to my feet and bend down to reach inside the hole, my fingers landing on a small tin pencil case my mother had gotten me from a yard sale. I pulled it out, staring down in disbelief at the rusted container in my hand.

Ella pushed to her feet and was now at my side, dusting the dirt from the back of her legs as she watched me. My heart was pounding in my chest as I opened the small box, forgotten for years.

Inside was a few trinkets from our secret relationship. A hair-tie with a small purple flower. I remember the day she pulled it from her hair, smiling as I ran my fingers through it. Another was a Polaroid picture we had taken together, her lips pressed against my cheek. Under the picture was a note, folded into a triangle.

Ella took the box from my hand as I stared down at the paper.

"What is it?"

"I have no idea." Shaking my head I slowly began to unfold the note. My eyes danced over the blue ink, immediately recognizing Katie's handwriting.

Ry,

I know you're probably really mad. You're the last person I ever wanted to hurt. I tried so hard to keep what was happening a secret. I was so scared I'd lose you or get sent away. Mom and coach came home early and caught Bryce trying to hurt me. I thought it was all over. I thought I could finally not be scared.

Bryce told them it was all my fault because I kept coming on to him. I told them everything but they didn't believe me.

Coach told me that if I said a word to anyone he would tell the school I was a whore and I was sleeping with you. He said he would tell everyone you were jealous of his son and trying to ruin his chance at a scholarship. I can't let them hurt you and I can't let them hurt me anymore.

My mother called my dad and told them they were sending me to live with him because I wouldn't leave Bryce alone. My father said he didn't want me and I was her problem. I don't want to be anyone's problem anymore.

I love you, Katie

I crumbled the paper in my fist as I thought over what I'd just discovered. Katie thought I'd be better off without her. She was all alone and thought I was ignoring her when she needed me most. Worse, her own parents betrayed her and I had the proof all of these years and didn't know it.

"What? What did it say?"

Turning to Ella, her eyes pleading with me for answers, I struggled to contain myself. "My *To Do* list just got longer."

Her eyebrows furrowed as she waited for answers, but I couldn't find the words to tell this girl that she had been betrayed by those who took her in, promised her a safe haven.

"Ella, everything I touch turns to shit." I turned away from her, wondering what would have happened had I discovered this note after Katie died. Everything would have been different. Ella had a shot at a normal childhood after being abandoned by her real parents. *Poison.* I destroyed everything, I was a plague. Now I had pulled Ella into my world and there was no way she would walk out of this unscathed.

I'd never be able to stop. Every layer of the story uncovered more deception and pain. I've had to walk away from Katie in this very spot and I didn't know if I would survive walking away from Ella too.

Her fingers wrapped around my bicep, turning me to face her. "What did it say? What did she tell you?"

My throat was dry, my heart crushed but I faked a smile, slipping the mask back into place. "She told me goodbye. She said she loved me."

Ella's expression softened as her fingers rubbed lightly over my arm. "That's great, Ryder."

"It's excruciating. We should go. It's getting late and we need to eat."

She nodded, unsure but followed behind me as I took the path from the woods to my father's car. There was no way I was going to escape what I had to do. I couldn't let Ella go down with me. The least I could do is put an end to her nightmares so she could have some semblance of a normal life.

We didn't speak the entire ride back to my parent's house. My mother had cooked meatloaf and was setting the table as we walked through the front door. She did a double take when she saw Ella.

"Ryder, what are you doing here?"

"I came back earlier, but you weren't here. I decided to take dad's car for a drive and show Ella around."

She nodded, setting down a plate in front of her chair. "You know that's your car, Ryder. That's what your dad wanted."

"That's what *you* wanted. It was his car."

She shook her head as she grabbed two extra plates from the cupboard. "Ryder, he was fixing up that car for you. It was going to be a graduation present. He used to go on and on about how you had to look the part if you were going to be a rock star."

"Why didn't you tell me this before?"

"You never came around, never answer calls."

I struggled not to show my anger. My mother was the reason I was gone for so many years. I always assumed she wanted me to stay gone. "You knew where I was for years. You could have come to visit."

Sighing heavily she used a spatula to cut the meatloaf into slices. "I couldn't look at my son in that place."

"Did you ever think of how it felt to be there, alone?"

"Ryder, you had plenty of friends. Look at your band." She smiled and I realized I wasn't the only one who wore a mask, pretending I was someone else. "Now sit and eat some food. Tell me how you met your... friend here." She gestured to the other chairs as Ella looked to me. I nodded, pulling out a seat for her and waiting for her to sit before sinking down into my own.

"Ella this is my mother Kirsten. Ella and I have mutual acquaintances."

"Ahh… well, it is nice to meet you."

"Nice to meet you too." Ella blushed as my mother dished a slice of the meatloaf onto her plate. "Thank you."

I knew my mother was dying to say something about her resemblance to Katie, but was biting her tongue. The front door opened and Mr. Thomas walked in, grumbling about a late meeting. When he stepped into the kitchen, he stopped, his mouth hanging open.

"Ryder?"

"The one and only."

He smiled, genuinely happy to see me. "Good to have you home, son." I rolled my neck, cracking it as I struggled not to correct him. Nodding, I took a bite of my food.

"Well, this is not such a bad day after all." He leaned down, kissing my mother on the cheek before taking his own seat and dishing out his food. "Who is your friend?"

"Ella, this is Stephen."

Dinner conversation was minimal. My mother asked questions about the band and where I had been since I'd gotten out. All I could think about was Bryce. Ella helped my mother clear the table as I disappear into my old bedroom. It hadn't changed since I'd left except there was no dirty laundry on the floor. Sinking down on the bed I tried to sort through my thoughts.

There was too much information to process and it was impossible to sit next to Ella, knowing she wasn't going to forgive me after I did what I needed to do. But I had no other choice. There was only one way I could make all of this right and it was to eliminate *all* of the evil from her life.

I composed myself and went back out into the kitchen to let my mother know I was exhausted but I would visit again soon.

Driving Down the winding back roads, Ella sat beside me, her hands in her lap, not saying a word. I reached out to the mirror and pulled the dream catcher from the cotter pin that held it in place, handing it to her.

"That one has his name on it."

She turned it over in her hands, running her fingers along the small webbing of the center. "How are you going to do it?"

I stretched the muscles in my neck as I turned onto interstate 95 north bound. "I'm not." I glanced over at her as I slid my hand into my pocket and pulled out the old pocket knife that I'd found in New Orleans. It was similar to the one that belonged to my father. I'd always planned on killing the Bryce the way his actions ultimately ended Katie's life. But Ella still had to live with the scars and the nightmares that plagued her.

I held the knife out and she took it, eyeing it curiously as she pulled the blade out of its casing. She pressed the tip of her finger against the point as she eyed her reflection in the blade.

"I don't think I can." She shook her head.

"You won't have to either. Bryce is going to kill himself." I drove off the exit ramp and travelled a few more miles down the road before pulling into a Best Western parking lot. "We should have a plan tonight."

Nodding she unbuckled her seat belt and pushed open her door.

I paid for a room, dying to get her alone, but there was work to be done and I needed to know exactly where Bryce and his family were now.

The room was larger than the others we'd stayed at in the past with a love seat and small table for two. The walls were beige and all of the furniture white, including the comforter on the king size bed. Ella kicked off her shoes, dropping her bag on the couch, pulling her purse strap over her head and dropping that as well.

"We should figure out how the day will go tomorrow so there are no surprises." She nodded, pulling the clip from her hair, my eyes lost in the dark waves. I dropped my bag on the floor and grabbed the hotel notepad and pen from the nightstand beside the bed. Now wasn't the time to be thinking about being inside of Ella. It was time to feed the other monster first.

I dropped the notepad on the table beside her. I need an address and directions. Tucking her hair behind her ear, she sat down on the chair, her leg bent underneath her. I gripped the back of the other chair as I watched her write.

"How did you get this?" I grabbed the pad and read over the address.

"Bryce liked to talk to me… after." She cringed and I struggled to not go after him right now.

Grinding my teeth, I forced myself to keep my composure for Ella's sake. "What did he say?"

"Ryder, you don't want to hear all of that."

Sinking to eye level I placed my fingers under her chin and forced her to look me in the eye. "I want to know *everything* he did to you so I can make sure he gets it worse than he *ever* gave it."

"He would talk about the things he wanted to do to me, these sick fantasies he saw online. He was going to take me to a place he rented down in Redmond."

"He doesn't have any properties in his name."

"It's a place a bunch of guys pay for and they each get a few weeks there a year."

"A timeshare?"

"Maybe. I don't know." Her shoulders slumped and I dropped my hand to her leg, rubbing over the bare flesh.

"It's okay. You're doing good. What about these other guys. Have you ever met them?"

"No. He never got the chance to take me there. I ran away after I ended up in the hospital."

"Good girl." I was dying inside but thankful that Bryce's friends never got their hands on Ella. "You're a fighter. I love that about you."

Her eyes widened and I immediately regretted my choice of words, but as her cheeks tinged pink I couldn't help but smile.

"I wasn't very good at fighting, hence the hospital." Rolling her eyes she adjusted in her seat.

"I promise you, Bryce won't win his next fight. He *will* pay for what he did."

"I'll just be glad when this is finally over."

I swallowed against the sudden dryness in my throat. Ella didn't know what this being over would entail but hopefully it would give her some peace and she'd be able to move on. She deserved to be a wife and mother, never having to look over her shoulder.

"Soon," I feigned a smile, desperate to keep my mask in place but it was slipping. I'd never shared so much with anyone, not even Katie. I was too ashamed to tell her about my father, afraid she'd leave me. "But I need to make sure I have all of the information you have, okay? We're almost done."

Standing up, I stretched and reached for her hand. She slid her fingers over my palm and I pulled her to her feet. I grabbed her bags from the small love seat and sat them on the floor before sitting down and pulling her down next to me. She turned her back to my side, leaning against me and keeping my arm around her waist.

"These other guys," clearing my throat I searched for the right way to phrase my question. "They do the things Bryce did to others?"

She shrugged and I hated that I couldn't see her expression but maybe it would be easier for her to open up without having to look me in the eye.

"I think so."

"You said he talked to them on the internet. Did he ever mention a website or a group?"

She began to squirm and I tightened my arm, not to keep her from moving, but to make her feel safe. Lowering my mouth next to her ear I whispered, "Anything that happened to you is on him. None of this is your fault. I'm here, sweetheart. It will be over soon."

"I only knew the name of one of the guys he talked about a lot. I searched the little bit of information I had to find the house. But I have no idea when he goes there or if he is staying there full time." She pulled from my grip and I let her go. She wrapped her arms around her stomach and began to pace. "What if he's not there?"

I pushed from the couch and stood in her path. "I will find him." She stopped abruptly, her eyes filled with uncertainty. "I'm sorry I lied to you about who I was."

She raised her hand slowly and brushed her fingertips across my temple and into my hair. "They are just things you've done, not who you are."

"You have no idea who I am. It's better that way."

"I know most people would have looked the other way in that alley, but you didn't. You *saved* me."

"I nearly killed that guy. I *would* have killed him if you weren't there. You were terrified... of *me*."

"I wasn't scared of you. I was scared of myself. I wanted him dead. I wanted him to suffer. He *deserved* to suffer."

I ran my hands through my hair as I turned away from her. "You didn't want that. Not really." I turned back to her. "Thinking it and doing it are two different things, Ella."

"You don't know what I want."

I nodded, swallowing back the lump in my throat. "I do," I reached up slowly and tucked her long hair behind her ear, letting my fingers trail over her cheek before it fell to my side. I looked down over tank top to her jogging shorts, desperate for the same thing, and no longer able to deny myself.

CHAPTER THIRTY

ELLA
INEVITABLE

Inevitable: Certain to happen; unavoidable.

His fingertips slid over the raised scars on my thigh and I closed my eyes, forcing myself to ignore the embarrassment that welled inside of me.

"We all have scars, Ella. Some of us just have them on the inside." His voice was gravelly and quiet. My body shivered as his warm breath blew over my ear.

"Where are yours?" I slowly opened my eyes as his long fingers wrapped around mine. He lifted my hand and placed it on his chest, directly over his heart. I could feel his pulse racing under my fingertips. The pained expression on his face mirrored what I was feeling inside. It was hard to let someone in, to trust them, when so many have let you down in the past.

I'd had sex with several men over the years, but letting them get to know me, to see the real me, was the hardest thing I'd ever done. I'd felt exposed, naked, under his gaze and I was still wearing every stitch of my clothing. The worst part of it all, I could feel him pulling back. The idea of letting him in and knowing the hurt is inevitable felt like I was hovering over a flame. The warmth comforting but it would soon become all consuming. It would eventually devour me, destroy me. But I couldn't walk away.

He took his free hand and slowly raised it, never breaking eye contact as he placed it on the center of my chest. My lips parted and shallow shaky breaths were the only sound we made. Soon we breathed in unison, heavier as gravity seemed to pull us closer together. I could taste the mint as his air became mine. His mouth opened wider and for a moment I thought he was going to kiss me but instead, he spoke.

"I want to see all of your scars, in the light."

"They're ugly," I tried to pull my hand from under his but he held it tightly against him.

"Nothing about you could ever be ugly."

I dropped my gaze to his chest and he bent his knees slightly to catch my eye again. "Nothing."

My teeth dug into the sensitive flesh of my lower lip as he let go of my hand and removed the other from my chest. His fingertips curled around the bottom of my shirt and he slowly began to raise it. I was glad he could no longer feel my heartbeat because it was pounding rapidly with every inch of my body that became exposed. The pad of his thumb lightly brushed against my skin and over my ribs as I struggled to control my breathing.

My mind raced with uncertainty, the panic spreading from my belly and winding its way through every fiber of my being. Ryder inched closer and pressed his forehead against mine and the voices were silenced. My eyes falling closed as I let myself be absorbed by him, to focus on his breathing that he had deliberately slowed. I matched my breaths to his and his hands began to move my shirt further, over my ribs. They went behind my back as he reached my shoulder blades.

I stepped back fractionally as he pulled it over my head, his eyes never dropping below my face.

"Are you okay?"

I nodded not being able to swallow past the lump that had formed in my throat. He dropped the shirt at his side and looped his fingers in the band of my shorts. Slowly, painfully slowly he dragged his fingers down my hips and over the tops of my thighs until the fabric fell free and dropped to my feet.

I was wearing nothing but a basic beige bra and teal underwear. "Had I known I wouldn't have worn something so plain," I laughed nervously and the side of his mouth pulled up into a smile.

"You look anything but plain." His eyes lowered as he looked over the small scars the marred my body. His expression never changing to anything but admiration. He didn't cringe at the extra thickness of my hips, or how my belly wasn't perfectly flat.

I summoned all of my courage and stepped forward, gripping the bottom of his shirt. I lifted it over the ridges of his abdomen, unable to look away from how perfectly sculpted his body was. What the hell could he possible see when he looks at me? This guy could land any women he wanted, no doubt he has in the past. As I reached his chest he grabbed the shirt and pulled it over his head, tossing it to the side.

I swallowed hard as I looked up at him. My fingers finding the button of his jeans. I tried to keep my fingers from shaking as I tried to undo them.

"This doesn't make you nervous at all?"

He laughed, his tongue running out over his lips that made my panties feel like they melted right off my flesh.

"This isn't who I am. That's in here." He tapped his fingertip against his temple. "And here." He placed his palm over his heart.

"You're braver than I am," I shook my head.

"You don't give yourself enough credit." His fingers slid over mine and I let my hands fall to my sides as he undid his pants and shoved them to the floor, stepping out of them. I glanced down at his boxers and laughed, my hand quickly covering my mouth. "What?" his smirk grew flashing perfect white teeth.

"Are you serious?" I pointed to his boxers and he feigned embarrassment.

"It's not polite to point at a man's crotch and laugh."

I was giggling uncontrollably. "Why is there a picture of an elephant head on your boxers?"

He glanced down at his boxers and shrugged. "It makes more sense when he has his trunk."

"How does it," my voice trailed off as momentary confusion turned to understanding and I began to laugh so hard tears ran down my cheeks.

"Alright. That's enough. Now I'm starting to regret taking my clothes off in front of you."

I held up my hand but I couldn't stop. No sounds was even coming out anymore as I doubled over.

He folded his arms over his chest and cocked his eyebrow as he waited for me to regain my composure.

CHAPTER THIRTY-ONE

RELLIK

ADORATION

Adoration: Deep love and respect.

I pretended to be upset but seeing Ella's eyes light up was all I had been dying to see since she came into my life. Her cheeks were bright red and for once the tears were out of happiness. "I found these in my old room. I thought you'd like them."

I put my hands on her hips and her giggles cut short. Leaning down, my mouth hovered over hers. "I could always take them off." Sliding my boxers over my hips, I kicked them to the side. "That better?"

She nodded, rocking on her toes. I knew she wanted me to kiss her but I didn't want to forget this moment of her looking at me with adoration.

"Why are you looking at me like that?"

"You're so beautiful," I mumbled as I pressed my lips to hers, the world evaporating around us as soon as we touched. I slid my fingers under her bra straps and pushed them off her shoulders as her hands went behind her back to unclasp. The bra fell down her arms and to the floor between us. She gripped her panties and slid them down her legs, kicking them to the side before pushing against my chest until my back of my legs hit the bed. I fell back with a chuckle and she climbed onto the bed, straddling me. She rolled her hips, rubbing her wetness along the length of my cock.

I groaned, my dick painfully stiff. Gripping her shoulders as I flipped her onto her back, my body pressing her into the mattress. My mouth found hers and I rocked my hips against her causing her to whimper. She shoved hard against my shoulder and I laughed, grabbing her hands and pinning them to the bed on either side of her head. She smirked, bucking her hips and biting down on my lower lip.

"Fuck," I let go of one of her hands and she pushed me off her. I slid off the side of the bed. She was daring me to chase her as she transferred her weight from foot to foot. "I'm going to make you pay for that." My eyes narrowed as she raised her eyebrow.

I dove to her side of the bed and climbed off the side as she squealed and ran toward the hotel door, but there was nowhere for her to hide. I wrapped my arms around her waist as she laughed hysterically.

"You think that's funny?' I spun her around, pressing her naked chest against the door, pinning her there as I entered her from behind. Here fingers were splayed on the door and I leaned forward, sliding my hand over hers and interlocking our fingers as my left hand gripped her hip. I fucked her hard, I pressed my cheek against hers loving the sound of us panting together. "That feel good, sweetheart?"

"Yes," she moaned, breathless.

"Tell me."

"You feel… so good… inside of me, Ryder."

I slammed into her again and again until her body began to tighten around me. I knew she was going to come soon.

"I think you were made for me, Ella."

"I'm yours, Ryder," she moaned and it sent me over the edge. I came hard as her body pulsed around my dick.

I wish I'd had the courage to tell her that it was the other way around. From the moment I saw Ella, I never had a chance.

CHAPTER THIRTY-TWO

ELLA
SECRET

**Secret: Not known or seen or not meant
to be known or seen by others.**

I rolled over, stretching in the mess of covers, my body deliciously sore from the night before. As I reached for Ryder, my hand fell on an empty pillow, causing me to sit up in a panic. It took a moment for my eyes to adjust in the darkness but it was very apparent I was alone.

"Ryder?" I jumped from the bed and turned on the light, momentarily blinded from the brightness. I grabbed my clothing scattered on the floor and began to pull them on quickly. I grabbed the hotel phone and quickly dialed his cell, desperate to hear his voice, but it went to a voice-mail that hadn't been set up. "Fuck." My eyes scanned the room and that's when I noticed his notebook that he had kept in his duffle bag on the table.

Picking it up I flipped it open to a page marked by the note Katie had left for him in the woods. My eyes scanned it, blurring with tears as I discovered the horrible truths of her secret. The Alexander's knew what was happening. They gave her no choice and they took me in knowing it would happen again. My hand went over my stomach as I dropped the letter on the table, my eyes focusing on the notebook page that had been marked.

I'll open your cage my sweet butterfly
One final page and all villains must die
Happy endings in reach but comes with a price
My love and my life are my sacrifice

I flipped the page, desperate more of his words but there was nothing. "He's going after her parents." I flew around the room, struggling to figure out what I could do. There must be something I can do to stop him. I had no idea how much of a head start he had on me, but I had to find him before I lost him.

I pulled open the zipper on his duffle bag and began pulling out his belongings until I found the small scrap of paper with the phone number I had seen before. My fingers shook as I grabbed the phone and dialed the number.

"What did you do," the deep voice, groggy from sleep asked and I recognized it immediately.

"Is this Phantom?" My voice cracked, afraid I was going to make things worse for Ryder, but I had no choice.

"How did you get this number? This is a burner phone." He sounded more alert now and pissed off.

"It was in Ryder's things. This... this is Ella, from the bar."

"I know who the fuck this is. Where is he? Why didn't he call me?"

My voice dropped to a whisper as I struggled with how much of the truth to share with him. Ryder made sure on Trigger knew I was still around and I wasn't sure if he kept his other side a secret as well. "He's in trouble."

The weight of the situation was crushing me, my heart struggling to beat against the fear. I told Phantom as little details as possible and he promised he was on his way to get me. Pacing the sidewalk outside of the hotel, I watched every vehicle that drove by, in hopes the next would be the guys.

When they finally pulled up, Trigger jumped out of the passenger seat and held it open for me. I slid in, thanking him as he closed the door and got in the back with Phantom. Hangman was behind the wheel and he took off as I gave him directions toward the Alexander's home.

"Explain what the hell is going on," Phantom snapped.

"Ryder... Rellik... ugh... is going after Katie's parents."

"He told you about Katie?"

"I already knew about her." I swallowed hard, rubbing my hands together nervously. I didn't want to rehash my past, I just wanted Ryder safe. "The Alexander's were my foster family."

"Holy shit," Hangman mumbled as he shook his head.

"Why the parents? Why now?" Trig leaned forward in the back seat.

I wiped a stray tear from my eye and cleared my throat as I held up the note. Trig took it, turning on one of the small overhead lights as he read it aloud. My heart broke all over again for Ryder as I pictured his face in the woods. He knew then he was going to leave me behind and last night was him telling me goodbye.

"Maybe we should call the police."

"No," Trig held the note out for me and I nodded in agreement. I always knew I'd have to face them again but I never thought it would be like this. "Whatever he plans to do, he is going to do. We won't be able to stop him."

"We have to stop him. We have to." I knew Ryder wasn't planning on getting away with anything. Had I not shown up in his life he would be oblivious to Bryce's whereabouts and the note left by Katie.

As we pulled up out front of the Alexander's home, I began to mumble under my breath, rapidly counting as every nerve in my body seemed to catch fire, fear settling deep in my belly as the panic attack began to take over. Ryder's car was parked right in front of us. It was the middle of the night but the living room light was on and I could see the movement of shadows behind the pale curtain. I waited for the others to get out before we crossed the street, time seeming to slow and I was thankful because I didn't want to know what was on the other side of those walls.

Phantom climbed the porch and pressed against the front door and it swung open, squeaking on its hinges. "Maybe you should wait out here."

"No," I pushed by him and he grabbed my wrists just as my eyes landed on Ryder, who sat in a chair, his elbows on his knees as he hung his head. I wished I could see his face, but I didn't need to when I saw Janet and Coach on the couch in front of him. They looked terrified but no one making a sound, no one but Macie who mumbled incoherently as Janet bounced her on her knee.

"Ryder," I whispered as I took a step closer, he shook his head but didn't move as he turned his pocket knife over in his hands.

"How could you do this to us," Janet called out and Ryder's head snapped up, the tension in the room palpable.

"How could you do this to Katie? To me?" I asked, jumping as Trigger placed his hand on my shoulder, encouraging me to be strong.

"What are you talking about? How dare you talk about my daughter?"

I held up the note, the paper shaking as I swallowed back my fear. "Katie left a note. You let Bryce hurt her. You let him hurt me."

I couldn't keep my eyes off Macie, her hair dark but short and big green eyes. I took another step until I was beside Ryder. "The baby." His voice was rough as if he'd been fighting back tears.

I glanced down at him, as his eyes met mine, filled with pain. "One of your scars." He wasn't asking. He already knew the truth.

My throat closed as my hand instinctively went to my lower stomach, to the largest of my scars from my C-section.

"Why didn't you tell me?"

"I didn't know you'd come here. You didn't tell me what Katie had said." I shook my head, fighting to keep my tears at bay. Had we both been honest we wouldn't be in this mess right now. I could only imagine this disgust he must feel for me knowing that I had a child with a monster like Bryce. "I thought you'd hate me," I whispered.

He stood slowly as he glanced to the family, unremorseful to the terror they felt. "What's her name?"

"Macie, after my grandmother."

"Go get her." He nodded slightly in their direction. I glanced down at the knife in his hand, the tendons in his arm tensed as he gripped it tightly. Macie was probably the only reason they were still alive. I walked slowly toward the couch, placing my hands under Macie's arms and fighting against Janet's grip before lifting her to my chest and hugging her tightly as I burst into tears. I dreamed for this moment for months, dying inside every day that I had to be away from her.

Macie began to whimper and I bounced her as I tried to keep her calm, tugging on her yellow nightgown.

CHAPTER THIRTY-THREE

RELLIK
INNOCENT

Innocent: Not guilty of a crime or offence.

I couldn't walk away from what had been done to Katie and Ella, but I'd never expected that from all this would come an innocent child. Ella held the baby tightly against her chest and there was no animosity, only love.

From all of this tragedy another life was created, and now I had to decide if I was going to take more away. I couldn't think clearly, couldn't contain the onslaught of emotions. The last thing I expected was to feel ambivalent toward those who had caused so much pain.

"Rellik, it's not too late to walk away," Phantom called out as Ella walked back toward the door.

"I promised Ella I would finish this."

"You have finished this," Phantom looked to Ella who was kissing Macie's head, whispering sweetly to her child.

"She won't ever feel safe until they're all gone."

"Ryder, I won't feel safe if I lose you." Her voice shook as she clutched her child tighter and I turned my attention to her. "You're my magic shield."

I shook my head, pressing the tip of the knife blade against my palm, my head spinning with doubt. "Ella, you deserve so much better and I deserve nothing. Macie deserves so much better than what I can give anyone."

"I love you." Her words cut through me, shredding any last hope of being able to walk away. With a thunderous clap the storm that had been brewing for all of these years was upon us as Ella spread her wings. Macie began to cry, Ella's eyes widened and I could feel the sensation of warmth on my chest.

Was this love? Excruciating pain radiated through my body in waves. My fingers went to my shirt, pulling back crimson-coated fingers as the color grew, bleeding out into the grey. My legs gave out and I fell to my knees, my eyes meeting Ella's who was frozen in terror. The muffled shouts and screams faded out around me as my eyes closed and I drifted off into my eternal nightmare.

CHAPTER THIRTY-FOUR

ELLA
LOVE

Love: An intense feeling of deep affection.

This was love. It was giving your heart to someone else with the understanding that it may be taken away.
I screamed, fingers clawing at my flesh as I begged to go to his side. Hangman wrapped his arms around me, cradling Macie and blocking me from danger.

Trigger wasted no time as he tackled Coach, struggling to disarm him. My eyes met Ryder's, his fading and mine wide. This was why he didn't want me to love him. He knew this feeling and wanted to spare me the agony. People die, but love doesn't waver.

Phantom was on his knees, hands against Ryder's chest as he fought to keep my love from leaving me. I couldn't breathe, not knowing his next breath may be his last.

Janet was screaming as another shot was fired. Everyone was shouting and soon the voices came from strangers as police swarmed inside the small home. Ryder was placed on a stretcher, his eyes closed as the rushed him out of the house and into a waiting ambulance.

"I need to go with him," I panicked as Hangman forced me to sit. Coach was wheeled by me on a stretcher, the white cloth that covered his body stained red like a Rorschach test.

I gave my statement as quickly as possible, handing over Katie's suicide note to the police. The fact that Ryder had been shot in the back ruled out self-defense. After they learned that Janet had been keeping my child from me and her knowledge of the abuse I'd endured, I was allowed to go to the hospital to be by Ryder's side. Janet was going to finally get what she deserved and it was only a matter of time before Bryce did as well.

I grabbed Macie's car seat from Janet's car and placed it in the back of the Barracuda, hurrying to get to the hospital. I couldn't fathom not being by Ryder's side when he was in so much pain. When I arrived, he was in emergency surgery and I couldn't get any information, just sad eyes and pity.

"She's beautiful. How old is she?" I glanced up at a nurse who stood by my side in heart covered scrubs.

"Almost two." I smiled at Macie as I stood her up on my knees.

"She looks just like you."

I ran my hands through Macie's messy hair, relieved that when I looked at her, I didn't see any of Bryce.

"Want to get her a snack? I have some diapers too if she needs changed."

I hesitated, looking down the hall. The guys hadn't arrived and it had been nearly two hours.

"Come on. I promise you'll know as soon as he is able to have visitors."

Reluctantly, I nodded and stood. The nurse put her hand on my shoulder and guided me towards the vending machines.

The nurse bought Macie a bag of gold cheesy fish and an apple juice. I changed her and sat her down in the waiting room, allowing her to eat her snack.

Just as I was able to rock Macie to sleep Ryder's mother and step-father walked through the door.

"Ella, what happened?" Kirsten's eyes danced over the baby on my lap.

"Ryder was helping me." I closed my eyes, hating that I'd have to live this nightmare again.

I broke down, giving as much detail as I could stomach, omitting anything that would reflect badly on Ryder. It was more than apparent Ryder still held a lot of resentment for being locked away. I didn't want to overstep and give more than he would want me to share.

CHAPTER THIRTY-FIVE

OBLIVION

**Oblivion: he state of being unaware or
unconscious of what is happening.**

I blinked awake, the light painful on my eyes and my
head swimming. I was high, my body liquid.

"Stay," a voice commanded as there was pressure against
my shoulder. I struggled against the force but couldn't
move.

"His vitals are good," another voice called out. "You
dodged a bullet, son. So to speak."

I drifted back off into oblivion but it wasn't Katie's
face I saw. I stared into Ella's wide, frightened eyes as she
thought she had lost me forever. Before that moment,
I'd never thought anyone would care if I'd died. Truth
be told, I thought they would be relieved, not having to
carry the burden of knowing me any longer. I lived with
reckless abandon, convinced that death would finally
cease the perpetual ache of losing the girl I loved. I
never thought it was possible to have that feeling again.
My heart was broken, but so was Ella's and those pieces

fit together. In my darkest hours, she found something in me to love, even when I couldn't love myself. In all of the evil I'd done, I'd somehow managed to save her and she would save me from myself.

"I love you."

Those words. Ella was the only reason my heart still had the will to beat. I couldn't leave it unsaid again. I needed to make sure she knew that I loved her.

I had no idea how much time had passed since I had been shot, but as my eyes blinked open all the pain in the world couldn't stop me from smiling at the sight of Ella. The fluorescent lighting overhead looked like a halo around her beautiful face. Perfect for the angel she was to me.

"You scared me," she sighed with a smile as her eyes clouded over with tears.

"I love you." I couldn't waste another minute without letting her know how I felt.

"I love you." She wrapped her thin fingers around mine and squeezed my hand.

I tried to sit up but the pain was too much and I groaned in agony as a nurse patted my left arm. "Don't try to get up just yet. Give your body time to heal."

"Where's Macie?" Panic began to set in as I realized Ella's arms were empty.

"Your mother is holding her." She glanced over her shoulder as my mother stepped forward.

"How are you feeling?" My mother asked as she rubbed her hand over Macie's back.

"Complete." I reached my hand out and my mother dipped lower so I could run my fingers over Macie's head.

My mother smiled as she took a step back and Phantom took her place next to me.

"You scared the hell out of us."

I sighed, not wanting to hear how I put our band on the line for Ella.

"But now I know why. Next time, call me first. I would have been there with you."

"I will." I nodded as I stared at Ella, unable to take my eyes off her.

"Alright, enough of this sappy shit." Hangman called from the foot of the bed and everyone laughed, easing the tension.

"Don't say shit in front of his mom, man." Trig slapped Hang on the chest.

"You just said shit in front of his mom too." He slapped him back and trig hit him in the back of the head.

"You just fucking said it again." Trig snapped and Ella got lost in a fit of giggles.

"Alright boys. This is a hospital." The nurse gave them a stern look with her fists on her hips. The both mumbled apologies as she shook her head. "Let's let Mr. Bentley sleep. He needs his rest."

I gripped Ella's hand so she wouldn't go as the others filed out of the room.

"You know how they say when you are close to death your life flashes before your eyes?"

"Yes."

"It's not true. All I saw was my future. All I saw was you and Macie. I won't ever put that in jeopardy again. I promise."

Epilogue

MONSTER

Monster: Ryder "Rellik" Bentley

It had been two years since I was shot, the wound long healed leaving behind a small scar that was a constant reminder of the moment Ella told me she loved me for the first time. The other events of that day faded into the background, letting my past remain where it belonged. Coach was dead, and Bryce committed suicide after hearing that his father had been killed and the police were looking for him. After hearing from Ella that the guys were missing from the hospital for a few hours, I didn't need to ask what happened to my pocket knife. Janet disappeared into a bottle of liquor and was forced to live after losing everyone. That was enough of a punishment for me.

After taking a few months off to recover we began to play local gigs again, occasionally travelling to visit the family of the other guys. But with Macie in Head Start, my family couldn't always travel with us. Luckily, my mom was always eager to babysit Macie whenever she got the chance.

Now that I had a family to take care of, I had to decide whether or not I wanted music to be my career or get a full time job with a reliable paycheck. I decided we could do both. Ryder Bentley was now the proud owner of Get Bent, the hottest new club in Orlando. We play there live every week as well as a few other up and coming local bands. There was even a story about my club and the changing of the music industry in Rolling Stone.

I was better at controlling my anger now, but Ella was still able to bring out my darker side, enjoying that monster she fell in love with.

"Get on the fucking bike, El. I'm not going to let you get hurt." I tried to hide my frustration, but my patience was running thin. She didn't trust me.

"I'm scared," Her voice wavered as she broke eye contact, looking over my black motorcycle.

"Of me or the bike?" I cocked my head to the side and her eyes narrowed. I could see her stubbornness begin to surface. She had too much pride. I was going to win this battle.

"Fine." She snatched the helmet from my hand. "Go slow," She ordered as she slid it over her head and strapped it in place. I rolled my eyes as I threw my leg over the bike and waited for her to join me.

She gripped on to my shirt as she climbed on behind me. I grabbed her arms and pulled them around my waist, her chest pushed against my back.

"You're going to go slow, right?" She spoke into my ear as I started the bike.

"Not a chance in hell."

"Then I'm getting off!" She yelled as she pulled back, but I grabbed her wrist and held it against my stomach.

"You want to get off, Ella, I can get you off." I pulled out before she could respond causing her to tighten her hold on me.

I couldn't stop smiling knowing that the rush off fear would turn her on and later we'd fight and fuck and I would get to hold her and love her. Fucked up people take pleasure in fucked up things. Ella was used to being afraid, she was used to having to fight. She loved challenging my need to control and she knew she no longer had anything to fear because the meanest fucking monster was hers. She'd tamed the beast and given me a reason to live. We weren't anywhere near perfect but we fit perfectly together.

THE END

PRETTY LITTLE THINGS

TERESA MUMMERT

"All things truly wicked start from innocence."

—Ernest Hemingway

Mara, you have no idea how awesome you are.

PROLOGUE

I was young enough not to understand that my life was different. Colin became the one person I could count on to protect me. He suffered for the both of us by carrying the burden of our secret.

We were the lucky few who got a chance to start over. A fake family, a new home, and a pretty little life built on lies. But while our lives continued to intertwine, we were put on very different paths. Now it was only a matter of time before they'd collide and the beast behind the beauty would be exposed.

Chapter One

Annie

I knocked on the office door that sat ajar as I watched Colin at his desk, his suit jacket off and sleeves rolled up, exposing the large cross tattoo on his forearm, as he stared at his laptop screen. His dark hair was disheveled, and a day's worth of stubble shadowed his jawline. Beside his laptop was a black gun that was always within reach.

"Busy," he snapped angrily, not bothering to glance in my direction as I glared at him.

"Good. I'll stay out of your way. Don't wait up." I turned to hurry down the flight of stairs toward the second floor, but he called after me before I could make my getaway.

"Wait. Where the hell are you going?"

I rolled my eyes and groaned like a child as I slowly traipsed back to his office and pushed the door open. "Out with some friends." His eyes ran up and down my body before he shook his head in disapproval, and his gaze dropped back to the computer screen.

"Not dressed like that. Go change."

"You don't get to tell me what to wear. I'm seventeen, and you're not my father." I folded my arms over my chest as my eyes narrowed, ready for a fight.

With a sigh, he pushed back his chair and slowly stood to his full six feet in height, making me feel impossibly small. He rounded the desk as he pulled up his zipper. That's when I noticed the mass of blond hair from a girl kneeling behind his desk. *Gross.* He came to a stop in front of me, forcing me to tilt my head back. It was challenging to glare at someone from this angle and still look menacing.

"Change your outfit, or you're not leaving."

"Watch me." I pivoted on my toes, my long blond curls hitting him in the chest. Two muscular arms banded around my waist, pulling my feet from the ground as he held me against him from behind.

"Annie, I'm a very fucking busy man," he growled next to my ear. "Do not pull this bullshit tonight. This is not a fucking game. Change your clothes, or I will lock you in your room. Do I make myself clear?"

"Crystal," I bit out between clenched teeth as he lowered me to the ground. To say Colin was overprotective of me was an understatement, but he was equally annoyed by my presence, which made dealing with him a constant game of Russian roulette.

"Asshole. You messed up my hair," I muttered as I made my way down to the second floor and into my bedroom. I slammed the door loud enough to rattle the walls, but I knew he probably didn't even hear it upstairs. That was one of the perks of living in such a large house. I glanced at my reflection in the full-length antique mirror across the room, running my finger under my lower lip to fix my smudged gloss. My hair was pale blond and curled perfectly down my back. I wore a low-cut purple V-neck

T-shirt that hugged my curves and made my green eyes pop, paired with cutoff jean shorts that probably cost more than the average person's week-long vacation. Well hidden and disguised was the credulous little girl that I used to be when we came to live in Connor's house.

I pulled off my shirt and tossed it on the ground as I stepped inside my walk-in closet. Pulling out a sensible white eyelet dress that covered anything Colin would find offensive, I cursed under my breath. I slid my shorts down over my hips and kicked them off against the wall as a knock came at my door.

"Go away," I yelled, and I heard the deep rumble of his laugh as he slowly opened the door and stepped inside my room. He had his hands shoved in his pockets as he looked me over in matching black bra and panties trimmed with delicate lace.

"I'm sorry. I have enough on my plate right now. With Connor sick, I have to pick up his work slack. I can't be worried about you running around town looking like…" He gestured with his hands, and for the first time since I could remember, Colin was at a loss for words as he took me in.

"I'm just hanging out with some friends. You guys want me to blend in; this was me blending in. No one at school dresses like this." I tossed my hands in the air, hating that at only nineteen he felt he could tell me what to do. He was taking his role as my pretend brother a little too far.

The loud clacking of heels on the wooden floor caught his attention, and he turned around to face *bobbing head from under desk* girl.

"I'll just be a minute, and then we can leave. You mind grabbing my keys from the office?"

"Sure." She smiled sweetly, her lips coated with a fresh layer of red, before disappearing up the stairs to the third floor. Colin turned his attention back to me, his jaw clenched in frustration.

"First of all, you wear uniforms at school. Second, you're a Blakely now. You need to dress the part. This is a very small town, and people talk. We've spent years trying to blend in, and now you want to walk around looking like a whore just to prove you're what? A grown-up?" His voice rose with every word, as did my temper. I crossed the room in large strides and poked my finger against his hard chest, but he didn't budge from the doorway, and the shadows from my darkened room made the chiseled contours of his face even more menacing.

"You don't seem to have a problem with the women you *fuck* dressing like whores. Why do I have to dress like a librarian?"

His hand was in my hair, fisting and tugging back ever so slightly, my chin titled up toward his face, which was now only an inch from mine. "If you don't dress like a lady, I will stop treating you like one, and that will be more fun for me than it is you, I promise." He swallowed hard, and my lips parted in shock as I struggled to keep my breathing under control. It wasn't a threat—it was a warning.

The hammering of my heart in my ears blocked out the sound of heels on hardwood, and it wasn't until *bobbing head from under desk* girl gasped, "Colin?" that we noticed her presence.

"Sorry, sweetheart. Just teaching my little sister here a lesson on being a lady." His body blocked her view of his hold on me as his eyes drifted to my chest. Then he pressed a kiss to my forehead, and his long fingers untangled from my hair. "*Now* I've messed up your hair," he whispered with a smirk.

"I'll be back." He stepped away from me, and I watched in shock as his perfect smile was in place. Wrapping his arm around the girl, they descend the stairs to the first floor. I leaned out of my bedroom doorway just as he glanced over his shoulder at me and winked.

I slammed my bedroom door hard and grabbed the white dress I had chosen, cursing under my breath as I pulled it over my head and ran my fingers through my now knotted hair.

I hurried down the flight of stairs and out the front door, stopping as my eyes caught sight of Colin, his body pressed against the *desk* girl, pinning her against the side of his car as his mouth moved along her neck.

I hurried down the steps and turned right, away from him. The property spanned miles and was bordered by a six-foot privacy fence, but through the woods there was a place where a few boards were missing. That was where I was headed. Barefoot and angry, I stomped my way through the trees, hurrying before Colin spotted where I was going.

When I reached the fence, I slipped between the missing slats and into Jacob's waiting arms. He smelled of smoke, weed, and sin. His hands slid around my lower back and began to creep down to my ass as he pressed his lips against mine. His body was thin but muscular like a swimmer. He was the only person in this town who didn't treat me like I was a fragile ornament whose only purpose was for decoration.

"You taste so good," he mumbled against my lips. I ran my hand over his dark hair, which was now long enough to always look like he'd just rolled out of bed. He pressed his lips against my forehead and pulled back to look at me. "Why are you dressed like a librarian?" His chocolate eyes were barely open under the weight of the drugs he'd consumed, and his lips twisted into a smile.

"Like you need to bother asking." I rolled my eyes, instantly infuriated all over again at being treated like a helpless child.

"I wish you'd let me talk to that asshole."

I took a step back and shook my head. Jacob and I had been seeing each other for three months, but no one else knew of our secret encounters. "I'd rather not subject you to his bullshit." I rolled my eyes as my fingers gripped the front of his dark-brown vintage T-shirt that read "Ramones" across his chest. But what I really meant, and what we both were thinking, was that no one would understand us. I didn't even know for sure what we were. Jacob had been a friend, and we'd blurred that line on more than one occasion, but I wasn't stupid. Our lives were very different. I was a Blakely, and he'd grown up in the wrong tax bracket. There was nothing logical or permanent about us.

He tucked a blond curl behind my ear, and I leaned my cheek against his warm palm.

"I can't wait to leave this horrible place and finally not have people telling me what to do."

Jake chuckled as he ran his hand over the back of his head. His lips curled up in the smile that made my knees go weak. "It's only horrible for one of us. You live on *that* side of the fence."

"The grass isn't always greener, Jake." I stepped forward and pressed my body against his as I laid my head against his chest.

"I'm just trying to give you some perspective. You don't have it that bad. And you know I have the greenest grass in town." His fingers slid into my hair, and he held me tightly, pressing a kiss to the top of my head.

Jacob wasn't the type of boy who was looking for a long-term relationship. He knew what to say to make me smile, and I pretended I was the only one he said them to.

"My dad is working late tonight. That girl who went missing a few weeks ago was found behind that run-down gas station off of Maple Street. We could watch a movie."

"You make crime sound so sexy," I deadpanned as I laced my fingers in his, and we began to walk out of the woods.

"Having a cop for a dad has its occasional perks."

"Like him looking the other way?" I sniffed the air, letting him know I could smell the pot all over him.

"If you ask me nicely, maybe I'll share." He winked, and the butterflies took flight in my stomach as we crossed the dirt road beside the field and made our way up his back porch steps. Jake's father was the local law and also an alcoholic who suffered from depression and a heavy hand, according to Jake. I'd never had the misfortune of meeting him and was happy to keep it that way. I had my fair share of dominant assholes in my life.

I stood inside the kitchen as Jake closed the door behind us. My eyes wandered over the mountain of unwashed dishes in the sink.

"You should really have someone do those."

"We can't all afford hired help, princess." He lifted my hand and pressed his lips against the back. I pulled my hand free from his and rolled my eyes.

"Don't call me that." I folded my arms over my chest as he chuckled, his fingers running through his messy dark hair.

"Aw…did I hurt your feelings?"

I turned my head away from him. "Please. I'd have to care for you to hurt my feelings."

"Ouch. Can I kiss it make it better?" He placed his fingertips under my chin and turned my face toward his. I couldn't contain the smile that spread across my face when I looked at him. "Is that a yes?"

He leaned forward slowly, his gaze falling from my eyes to my lips before he kissed me, softly. His mouth moved against mine, and I placed my hands on his chest as my lips parted. I pulled back, opening my eyes as I gazed up at him. "Is *this* why you brought me here? Just so you can try to get in my pants?"

"You're not wearing pants." He smirked as he took a step back and grabbed my hand, pulling me into the living room. "I'm picking the movie. That teenage drama shit put me to sleep last time. Happily ever after is for fairy tales and the delusional masses."

"*Hell on Main Street* kept me awake for two days. *I* pick."

He sat down on the couch, propping his foot up on the coffee table next to a stack of manila folders. He patted the cushion beside him, and I grinned as I sat down, our sides pressed together.

"I'll let you choose *if* you smoke with me."

"You know I don't like that stuff. It makes you stupid." I laughed, my hand over my mouth as he scowled at me.

"This coming from the girl who is in a guy's house, alone, in the middle of the night, and no one knows where you are?"

"Aw…" I grabbed the remote from the cushion beside me and turned on the television, flipping through the channels while Jacob stretched his leg to dig in his jeans pocket for his cigarette pack.

"What are you doing?" I asked as I tucked my hair behind my ear and continued to change channels.

"We had a deal, remember?"

"You can't smoke in here." I glanced down at the joint he had just pulled from the pack and shook my head. "Your dad is a cop. What if he comes home? My first time meeting your family is going to land me in jail."

He shrugged as he placed it between his lips and lit the lighter. I folded my arms over my stomach as I shook my head, which was now enveloped in a cloud of smoke.

"Come here." Jake's fingers slid along my jaw, turning my face to his as his mouth inched closer to mine. I let my lips part as he slowly exhaled, his smoke pouring deep into my lungs.

I held in my breath as my chest began to burn, and I coughed, a giggle escaping me as Jacob's lips curled into a mischievous grin. My cheeks heated under his gaze as his tongue rolled out over his lower lip.

"What?" I asked, my head tilted as I watched his eyes study me, feeling a blush creep over my cheeks.

"I feel like I'm corrupting you." He shook his head, but his gaze settled on my legs and slowly drifted upward. I smoothed my hands over the skirt of my dress, feeling naked under his scrutinizing gaze. But this was what I'd been wanting, someone who didn't want me to be perfect.

"I'd have to be innocent for you to corrupt me." My fingers grasped the hem of my skirt, and I slid it up my thigh an inch, watching as the column of his throat jumped from a hard swallow. He placed his hand over mine, lacing our fingers before pulling it to his face and pressing a soft kiss to my skin.

"You're such a tease."

I felt oddly comforted by the fact that he didn't want to use me to get in my pants, and I didn't need to be a mindless bimbo like all of the other girls in town. I leaned my head against his shoulder as he took the remote from my hand and flipped through the channels. "Let's do something for your birthday. Let me make you a cake or"—he laughed—"buy you a cake or something."

I smiled at his thoughtfulness. "I wish I could, but I'm having dinner with my family." The truth was I wasn't even sure anyone remembered, but to say it out loud was too embarrassing.

He pressed his lips to the top of my head, and with a heavy sigh I let my eyes fall closed.

The next thing I remember was waking up, my mouth tasting like it was full of cotton. Jacob was lying sideways, his legs off the couch, and I was resting my head on his chest.

"Shit!" I pushed up from him, wiping the hair from my face.

"What? What's wrong?" He pushed up on his elbows and rubbed his eye with the heel of his hand as he blinked away his exhaustion.

"Shit. Shit. Shit. What time is it?" I combed my fingers through my messy hair, my eyes darting around the dark room. The television was now playing a workout infomercial. "I have to go." I pushed against Jake's legs to move him out of my way so I could get off the couch without straddling his body.

"Let me walk you." He yawned through his words as he sat up, resting his elbows on his knees as he shook his head.

"No. Go back to sleep. I'll be fine." I turned to leave, but his fingers looped around my wrist, and I almost tumbled backward onto his lap. "Jake, I have to go."

"I'm walking you to the fence."

I twisted around to look at his face, which was illuminated by the television. He wasn't in the mood to argue, and neither was I. "All right. Hurry up."

Jacob pushed from the couch and put his hands on my hips from behind as he guided me from the house and out to the old field. I laced my fingers with his and gazed up at his beautiful face in the moonlight. He made my heart stop and race at the same time. The hard lines of his jaw, nose, and cheekbones made him look like he was carved from granite. His eyes looked black as coal, a stark contrast to his pale skin.

"When are you coming to see me again?" he asked, his eyes searching over my face.

"Depends on whether or not I get caught sneaking in," I laughed, but it was out of nervousness. I was not in the mood for Colin's bullshit. If he found out I was sneaking around with Jacob, I'd never hear the end of it.

I slowed as we reached the fence, not wanting to leave his side.

"Come see me tomorrow." He tugged on my hand, turning me to face him.

"It may be a few days."

He nodded as he gazed out to the fence. "You want me to walk you to your house?"

"I'll be fine. It's private property. I'm the only one who ever goes in those woods." I gripped the front of his Ramones T-shirt and pressed my mouth against his, letting my lips linger. As I pulled back, Jake's eyes slowly opened, and he grinned his heart-stopping crooked smile, his dark eyes hooded.

"I'll see you later." He ran his hand over his hair, causing it to stick up in every direction.

"Bye." I waved as I slipped through the hole in the fence and disappeared into the trees toward my home.

CHAPTER TWO

COLIN

I drained my double shot of Jim Beam down my throat, the burn long gone and replaced by numbness an hour ago. I looked down at my watch, but it was too dark to see the time, which was probably for the best because it would only enrage me further. It was three in the morning last time I'd checked. Annie hadn't called or texted, but her best friend Mara, whom she was supposed to be out with, had stopped by four hours ago looking for her.

When I heard the doorknob turn, I sat holding my empty glass in the formal living room, veiled in shadows. She stepped inside, walking on her tiptoes as she shut the door behind her, flinching as it clicked loudly into the lock and echoed throughout the cavernous space. She tiptoed to the stairs and grabbed hold of the banister.

"Is this fun for you?" I asked, and she jumped, grabbing her chest as she turned toward the sound of my voice, her eyes narrowed as she searched me out.

"Could you be more dramatic?" she whisper-yelled, not wanting to disturb Connor from his sleep, even though his room was on the third floor and he slept like the dead.

"More dramatic?" I asked as I pushed to my feet. I hurled the glass across the room, and it connected with the inside of the living room wall, shattering into the darkness. "That better?" I asked, arms stretched out at my sides as I walked toward her.

Her hands went over her face reflexively, and as she lowered them she stared daggers at me. "I don't have to listen to you."

"That so? Where were you?" I hurried toward her angrily. My filter had disintegrated with each drink, and now I was dangling from the edge of aggression.

"None of your business," she snapped and took off up the steps to avoid me, slipping and coming down hard on her knee, the cracking sound enough to cause me to flinch. She let out a cry of pain as she clutched at her leg, her body splayed on the staircase like a broken doll. *This is what happens to girls who get too close to me.*

I took the first three steps in one stride and lifted her effortlessly into my arms to carry her up to her room. "Fuck, Annabel," I groaned as we made it to the darkened hall above, and I kicked open her door with my foot. She cried, her tears wetting my bare chest. I laid her in the center of her bed and brushed the hair from her face, causing her to flinch and clutch her cheek.

"You hit your face?" Through the moonlight coming in through her window, I could see her nod, and the shadow of a forming bruise was already evident. "Hold on." I hurried back downstairs and grabbed an ice pack from the freezer, wrapping it in a red dish towel. When I made it back to her room, she was lying on her side, her hand on her face. I pulled her fingers away and pressed the ice pack to her cheek. She flinched, but her hand slid over mine to hold it in place. I stood up and sighed as I ran my hand over my dark, short hair.

"Thank you," she whimpered, sounding years younger than seventeen and more like that girl I had met a lifetime ago.

"Don't thank me yet. You're still going to tell me where you were."

"I was out with friends."

"You need to trust me and let me protect you. It's my job."

"I don't need you to protect me, Colin. I just want you to leave me alone." She rolled farther away, and the pain of her words hurt worse than a physical blow could inflict.

"Because you're so good at taking care of yourself? Look at you? You just kicked your own ass."

"I don't need to protect myself," she bit back, her feelings hurt from my implication that she was helpless.

That was it. That's what I was waiting to hear. She had met someone, and I had no idea who this guy was, and the fact that she smelled like marijuana did not get by me. The once perfect and innocent Annabel was falling from grace, hell-bent on proving me wrong about who she was. "You can continue to pretend that our life before we moved here was all just a bad dream. I *wish* I had that luxury. But I know exactly what happens to girls like you who think they are invincible."

"Yeah? What's that?" she challenged.

"I prove them wrong."

She rolled over halfway to face me in the dark. "Go away, Colin."

I stared at her shadowed silhouette for a moment before forcing myself to leave the room, pulling the door closed behind me but not latching it. My room was directly across the hall, and I slipped inside, leaving it wide open. I slid my dark suit pants down and kicked them off, falling onto my bed in only my gray boxer briefs. I could hear Annie's muffled cries from across the hall, and it killed me inside that I couldn't help her, that I couldn't trust myself.

When her sobs subsided, I was able to drift off into a nightmare-filled sleep, plagued by memories of a youth spent in hell. I was thankful Annie was able to block it out enough that she could project the appearance of functioning normally, but I knew it ate her up inside as much as it did me. I would gladly hold the weight of our troubled past if it meant she would have a normal future. Watching her slowly throw it away killed me inside.

I watched as Taylor's hand came down hard across Marie's cheek, and the sound of her grunt echoed in the large room as she fell to her side, catching herself on her hip and hands. Her strawberry blond hair covered her tear-soaked face. He straightened his tie and cleared his throat as he looked over at me. "Disobedience will not be tolerated." I nodded and watched the girl, a few years older than me but half my size, lie helpless and sobbing on the floor. It was a scenario I'd seen play out dozens of times. It no longer fazed me. It was the way things were. Every story was different and the same. This girl was a runaway who prostituted herself out in order to score drugs. I didn't know why Taylor even bothered bringing her in, but she fit the profile—blond hair and green eyes laced with flecks of gold—and he was becoming desperate to bring validity to his visions. The church was growing restless.

You either accepted the rules or you were beaten into submission, and Taylor was very creative with his punishments. I carried the scars on my flesh to prove it. "Pay close attention, boy."

I nodded once and waited. He grabbed Marie's arm and jerked her to her feet, giving her a second to regain her balance. I was sure that by morning her hip would be bruised, and simple acts such as walking would be difficult.

At fourteen, I was now being taught the inner workings of the church in order to prepare me for the day I would take Taylor's place. All encounters were videotaped for church records, something I never batted an eye at because it was just the way it was. To say my upbringing was unconventional was an understatement. The Descendants of God was a country-wide organization, and I was living at the epicenter and learning directly from our founder himself, Taylor Woodward.

He unfastened his belt as Marie wrapped her arms around her waist, sobs ripping from her chest.

"Don't hit me." Her pleading fell on deaf ears. I was no longer swayed by other people's pain. My empathy had long evaporated with every scar I received. Bad things didn't just happen to bad people. This was a fact.

He reached out and ran his thumb over her cheek to wipe away her tears. "Shh, I wasn't going to hit you. Praying isn't the only thing you will do on your knees around here." Her gaze fell lower, and she watched as he undid his pants. I glanced at the red light on the camera that sat in the corner of the room atop a tripod and kept *my expression unreadable, not wanting Taylor to see how much this still bothered me when he reviewed the tape. The only thing worse than the depraved acts I was forced to witness was having our leader deem me useless. I'd seen what happened to those who didn't conform, and I wasn't ready to meet my maker.*

I awoke to my mattress being nudged. My eyes flew open, and I stared up at Annie's messy, wild hair from a night of restless sleep. She was wearing one of my white undershirts, and it fell to midthigh. Mascara was smudged under her eyes from a late night.

"What's wrong?" I groaned as I blinked back the harsh sunlight that poured through my window. Annie's blurry image slowly came into focus. She held out a bottle of water and two pills in the other hand. I grabbed my covers and pulled them up, suddenly realizing it was morning and I was only in my underwear. The evidence of my twisted, fucked-up past was painfully hard, and control was something I lacked when I needed release. "Fuck, you could have knocked," I snapped.

"You could close your door if you want me to knock." She laughed as she set the bottle of water on my bare chest. The cold made me jump, and I sat up, my head thumping with the sudden movement. "Here."

I held out my hand, and she dropped the pills into my palm before tucking her hair behind her ear and sitting down on the edge of my bed with one leg tucked under her.

I swallowed them down and drank the bottle of water in one long sip. Her eyebrow rose as she watched me and shook her head. I rubbed the heels of my hands over my eyes and looked over at her, taking in the purpling of her cheekbone on her otherwise perfect porcelain skin.

"Shit," I groaned and reached out to run the pad of my finger over the mark, but she pulled back and swatted my hand away. "I'm sorry."

"It's not your fault. I'm fine." Just like that she shrugged it off as if it had never happened. Had her face not bore the mark of the encounter, it would have been erased from her memory entirely. That was what I envied about Annabel. She could block out anything that caused her pain and live in a bubble of contentment. That was why our new life suited her so well. She was a chameleon with a self-imposed dementia.

I shook my head as I sat up farther and ran my hand over the ridges of my abdominal muscles. "Is Grace making breakfast?"

Annie snorted and then laughed at herself. "She did an hour ago."

I groaned, and she rolled her eyes.

"I woke up late too. I had her save our plates, but you may want to get dressed. Amanda stopped by. You're welcome." She grinned and pushed from the bed.

"Fuck." I fell back and pressed the palms of my hands against my eyes as she left the room. I felt like shit, and I probably looked worse. "Take off my damn shirt," I yelled after her.

I pushed from my bed, glancing at the full-length mirror on the opposing wall. Working out had become one of the few ways to deal with my growing aggression, and the results were proof that I harbored a lot of rage. My muscles were cut, and I barely had any excess fat, but

I still wanted to be bigger, stronger. I was glad my scars only marred my back, and I wasn't forced to look at the physical manifestation of my sins and my early reluctance to obey Taylor.

I turned on the radio and sang along to "Outside" by Staind as I shoved down my boxer briefs, kicking them off on the floor. I made my way into my bathroom, turning on the light above the sink but leaving the one in the shower stall off to spare myself the harsh light. The water didn't take long to heat up, and I slid under the spray, closing the fogged glass door behind me.

I dumped liquid body wash in the palm of my hand and rubbed the soap over my chest and down my stomach as I begged for the adrenaline of my nightmares to subside. My hand dipped lower, knowing there was only one way to make those memories fade, and I wasn't proud of that fact. I gripped my dick, squeezing hard as my hand slid slowly up and down my length. I rested my forehead against the damp sandstone tile and closed my eyes, hoping I could find some sort of release.

The song ended, and waiting for the next to start was quickly killing my mood. Nine Inch Nails faded in through the speakers that were embedded above the shower stall, and I began to stroke myself faster as I pictured small, perky tits with light-pink pebbled nipples. I licked my lips as I focused on the faceless vision, my eyes traveling down a tight stomach while my fingers slipped over my head and back against the base of my cock. I panted, water droplets falling from my lips as I imagined it was swollen pink lips wrapped around me, sucking as my fist gripped her hair, tiny moans in the back of her throat vibrating and nearly sending me over the edge as I pushed her closer, touching the back of her throat with my dick.

"Ah…" I groaned over the music. I imagined her moaning my name, begging for me to come in her pretty little mouth.

"Colin?" Annie's voice came from inside my room.

"Fuck," I growled, but I was too close to be able to stop myself as my stomach muscles tightened.

"Colin?" she called again as she got closer, and it sent me over the edge.

"Fuck, Annie," I panted as I came, struggling to catch my breath as I stared at her emerald eyes through the fogged glass door. She didn't move for a moment, her lips parted in complete shock and breathing as erratically as me.

"Your shirt," she whispered as it fell from her fingertips, pooling at her feet, and her eyes locked on mine.

"Leave," I barked. My words jarred her, and she ran from my room.

I took my time drying off and getting dressed, not wanting to look Annie in the eye after what she had witnessed. I couldn't get the image of her out of my head.

I stumbled down the stairs in a black T-shirt and jeans, greeted by Amanda at the base of the steps. We'd been seeing each other for a few weeks. I kissed her cheeks as my eyes searched out Annie. She was standing in the doorway of the dining room wearing the low-cut purple V-neck from last night. Her blatant act of defiance struck a nerve deep inside of me, and she knew it. She was fucking with me.

"I'd watch for pieces of glass in your eggs. Grace isn't very happy with you," Annie teased, and I was relieved she wasn't traumatized by what she had witnessed moments before.

"I told your sister I'd help her cover up that bruise after we ate. She really shouldn't be allowed to walk in heels." Amanda stood on her toes to kiss my cheek as I glanced behind me at Annie again, with her tarnished complexion and her still bare feet from last night.

"Just don't paint her up. She doesn't need all that shit on her face." I tried to keep the harshness from my tone, but when it came to Annie, my judgment became clouded.

Amanda smacked my chest playfully, but she always wore more makeup than I liked. Most of it stemmed from her being self-conscious. Not that it mattered. She suited my needs.

I walked around Amanda and sat down at the large, ornately carved dining room table that looked like something right out of a castle. Connor was frivolous with his cash, something I would have to spend years correcting should his fortune ever get handed down to his pretend children.

Grace set my plate down with more force than necessary as she narrowed her eyes, accentuating the crow's-feet in her olive skin.

"Grace," I called after her as she retreated into the kitchen. "I'm sorry, sweetheart. It slipped."

"Mm-hmm," was all she said as she disappeared. At nearly sixty years old, she had no patience for my bullshit. Her snow-colored hair was pinned up in a neat bun. She wore a gray dress made out of what looked like burlap, with a white apron tied around her waist. I'd never seen her in anything else.

The woman must have aged twenty years from putting up with our bullshit. Connor had hired her only a week after he took us in; never having children of his own, he wanted Annie to have a woman around. Grace was more of a grandmother figure, and she played the role like one off a sitcom.

Amanda sat down beside me, her denim skirt riding up her thighs as she stole a piece of my toast and took a bite. Her hair was even blonder than the last time I'd seen her, and I wondered how many more trips to the salon before it was whiter than Grace's. "I love that shirt," Amanda said to Annie. I couldn't help but laugh as I glanced over at her, and she winked, proving her point about my choice of women.

I folded my hands in front of me and looked to Annie, who dropped her fork on her plate and clasped her hands together, annoyed but knowing better than to say so. This was a ritual that carried over from our past and was so ingrained in who I was that I would continue to do it, regardless of my feelings, or lack thereof, toward the commune.

"Dear Lord, thank you for this wonderful food and shelter you have provided us. We ask you, Lord, to help Annie fight back against the evil staircase and to protect her from any other inanimate objects that may bring harm her way, and Lord, please bless her with some clothes that actually fit her."

"Asshole," Annie groaned, and I tried to fight back a smile, clearing my throat as I opened my eyes. I shoved a bite of scrambled eggs in my mouth, relieved that Grace hadn't actually put any glass shards in my food, although I couldn't have blamed her.

I could hear Connor coughing off in the distance as he made his way to the first floor, the stairs creaking under his expanding weight. We glanced back at him as he entered the dining room, taking a seat at the head of the table. My eyes drifted over his charcoal suit, and I shook my head. "You're going to work?" I asked, knowing he was too sick, but the man had priorities, I had to give him that.

He cleared his throat as Grace brought in a mug of coffee and set it down in front of him. "Thank you, dear." He picked it up and took a sip before his eyes landed on mine. "Someone needs to pay for all of this stuff. I have cases that are piling up." But I knew he had become obsessive with his work when his wife had passed away nearly twenty years ago. He had confessed to me one night, not long after we arrived, that helping others helped ebb the guilt from not being able to do more for her as cancer slowly destroyed their lives.

"It wouldn't kill you to take a few days off, Connor. Enjoy life a little." I took a sip of my orange juice, my head still throbbing from my hangover. I'd tried, unsuccessfully, for months to get him to take a vacation. He deserved it for putting up with us for the last few years. The man was a saint. I wanted to help him in any way I could, but he wouldn't budge.

"I'll be in Jackson for Annie's birthday. I need you to keep an eye on the house. Don't let things get too out of hand." He changed the subject as the girls continued to eat their food.

"I'm sure Grace will keep everyone in line. No one can put the fear of God into someone like she can," I joked.

"Except for you." Connor was expressionless as he glanced at me over the rim of his cup, and my eyes narrowed. He didn't know the half of it.

"I don't get paid nearly enough for that task," Grace teased as she sat in one of the empty chairs with a bowl of oatmeal for herself and a freshly sliced peach on a saucer. "I'll be going with him to make sure he's getting plenty of rest and taking his medicine. I better not come back to a mess, ya hear?" She took care of Connor like he was her husband, but their relationship was strictly platonic, even though it would do them both some good to enjoy life a little. Still, it made me smile to know she was spending extra time with him, even if it was because of the flu.

"We'll keep the party low-key. Just a few friends." I laughed as I shook my head, knowing it would be out of control. Everyone at Annie's school, West Haven Private Academy, was dying to get inside our house, as well as everyone from Dyer Public.

"What party? I don't want a party. I'm not leaving this house until my bruise goes away. I look hideous." Annie rolled her eyes as she scrunched her nose.

"Oh, honey. You have to have a party. The town will be talking about it the rest of the year. The Blakelys are royalty." Amanda was grinning as she clasped her hands together in front of her teal polo shirt. No doubt she was thinking of the day I would ask her to marry me so she could be one of the elite. She would be waiting a long fucking time. She was oblivious to the circumstances that had brought us into this lavish estate or the endless line of women who filed through the door.

"The party is happening, and you don't need to worry about leaving the house because we're having it here." I raised my eyebrow at Annie. She glanced up at me and looked back down at her plate. Her cheeks tinged pink next to the purple mark. I knew she had thought we had forgotten.

"What happened to your face?" Annie looked at me before looking to Connor, who was leaning toward her, his elbows on either side of his plate. He was just as over-protective of her as I was, and I was glad I wouldn't carry the burden of keeping her safe alone.

"I slipped going up the stairs."

"You are as graceful as a newborn fawn," he joked, but his smile didn't reach his eyes as his gaze fell to me questioningly. It was a fair judgment on his part. He cared for us equally, but I could take care of myself.

"Being chased by a lion," she muttered as she glared up at me, and I shook my head, trying not to laugh.

I cleared my throat as I pushed my eggs around my plate. "I thought you needed to go to Jasper for the Raymond case? It's a slam dunk with the doctor's deposition."

Connor looked up at me, his eyes settling on Amanda momentarily. "This is a...private matter."

I sat straight up as I clenched my jaw and avoided Annie's questioning stare as I shoveled a bite of food into my mouth. I swallowed hard as I chose my words carefully. "I should go with you. I can't learn the business if you don't let me tag along every once in a while."

Connor laughed nervously as he wiped his mouth with the crimson cloth napkin. "You need to be here for Annabel's party. It's a big day. You'll get your chance soon enough." He smiled warmly over at Annie, who had her eyebrows drawn together. "Well, I should get my bags together. Grace?" He coughed as he pushed his chair back.

"I'll be right up." Grace collected her dishes and carried them into the kitchen as I ran my hand roughly over my jaw. "Ya'll better go on and get ready. You don't want to be late for church. God sees everything." Even knowing about our past, Grace refused to let us blame God. From the first day she arrived, she told us stories from the Bible and how God had given her so much even though we were her only family. Her positive outlook in even the bleakest situations baffled me, but I admired her for it.

"Wouldn't want that." Annie rolled her eyes as she stood and stretched. I'd never met a girl as stubborn as her and so dead set on being defiant; it was almost adorable if it wasn't so damn infuriating.

"I'll grab my makeup bag from the car." Amanda stood and bounded down the hall to the front door.

"You're not going to church in that outfit." I drummed my fingers against the wooden table as she got up and walked behind me toward the stairs.

"Who's going to stop me?" she whispered as she continued by.

"Annabel, wait." She paused as I pushed from my seat and walked toward her, sipping my orange juice as I approached her. "We need to clear something up."

Her eyebrows pulled together, and I knew her mind was replaying her walking into my bathroom because her cheeks flushed and her gaze fell.

"What I meant to say was change your *fucking* clothes *now*." I tilted the glass toward her, and she shrieked as the cold liquid soaked through her shirt onto her skin.

"You son of a bitch!"

Thirty minutes later, Annie came from her room in a sensible white button-up blouse and black pencil skirt. Her hair was curled perfectly down her back, and there were no traces of the bruise on her face.

We drove my car, a black 300S, to the church. It was just Annie and me. Amanda wasn't very religious, and I preferred this time to be just the two of us. Church in the South was very much a social event, and our presence was always required to represent the Blakelys.

Annie's fingers ran over the leather cover of her Bible as she stared out the window, watching the world going by, determined to give me the silent treatment. I reached up and turned down the volume of the radio. "You want to talk about the elephant in the room?" I asked. She raised an eyebrow as her gaze fell to my lap.

"I'd hardly compare you to an elephant," she deadpanned.

I laughed as I shook my head. "Now you're just being cruel."

"I learned from the master." She blushed and turned her gaze back to her window as I turned the radio back up. We drove a few more blocks before turning into Holy Trinity's gravel parking lot. I put the car in park and turned to Annie, who was still lost in thought.

"Hey." I touched her leg, and she jumped. "You all right?"

"Yeah." She tucked her hair behind her ear with a nervous smile. "I still don't really like these places." She shrugged, and I smiled sadly at her.

"This is a long way from the commune."

Her eyes searched mine before she nodded.

"Good girl. Let's go." I got out of the car and rounded the front of the vehicle, pulling open Annie's door. I held out my hand, and she slid her fingers against mine as I pulled her to her feet.

I put my hand on the small of her back as I guided her toward the door. We were greeted warmly by everyone we passed. Inside, the church was small but air-conditioned and well maintained. I preferred this to the megachurches you see on television. This was more personal, hands on, although not to the degree I was used to.

Annie and I slid into the back pew as she clutched her Bible on her lap. "You forgot your book."

"Never." I tapped my finger on the side of my head and winked. She shook her head and suppressed a giggle as the other members found their seats. I cleared my throat to keep myself from laughing as I nodded hello to Shelly Kline. She'd had her eye on me for a year, and it took everything I had to avoid her advances.

"She likes you," Annie whispered a little too loudly, and Ms. Baker turned around to give us a disapproving glare.

"She's not my type."

The service was short and to the point. The preacher spoke about sin and redemption. Before I knew it, we were back on the road speeding toward home.

"Do you believe all of that?" Annie asked, and her gaze cut to me.

"Believe what?" I asked, my eyes focused on the road ahead.

"That sins can just be wiped away? That you can do anything you want and there are no real consequences as long as you ask for forgiveness?"

There was a pregnant pause as I thought over her question. Was she asking for herself? Was she contemplating committing a sin, or was this about acts committed against her? "Some things are unforgivable, little one."

Her eyes narrowed, and I felt her gaze burning into me. "Do you still...believe in God?"

I looked over at her angelic face, the innocence still lurking beneath her toughened outer shell. "Yes." I reached for the radio and turned up the volume to end our conversation.

"She's the one, Colin. She's the one who came to me in my vision." Taylor was wildly animated as he dug through the pile of papers on his desk, searching for something.

"You say that about all the new girls." I tried not to sound bored, but this conversation was getting redundant, and I was growing tired of our monotonous routine. Taylor would bring a new family into our church and force them to live by his standards, only to molest and abuse their children.

"This one is a pretty little thing. You'll like her. Her name is Annabel."

He spent years trying to mold me into him, but he only succeeded in wearing away at my conscience until sick and twisted perversions were the only thing that made me feel at all. It didn't matter to me in whose name I acted.

"She is yours. A gift from God himself."

FOL

APR 0 2 2024

Made in the USA
Lexington, KY
28 October 2014